Fold Wormhole

Ron Mueller

Fold Wormhole

<u>Books and Stories by Ron Mueller</u>

<u>The Taelo Series</u>

Taelo: The Early Years
Taelo: The Golden Feather
Taelo: Journey of Discovery
Taelo: Dangerous Passage
Taelo: Condor Clan Slingers
Taelo: Circumvention
Taelo: The Journey of Sages
Taelo: Collection
Taelo: Future Leaders Journey

<u>A Taelo Story:</u>

White Swan and Quiet Pheasant
The Child's Name
Floating Cloud
Quiet Rabbit
Busy Bee
Little Otter & Talking Wren
Broken Spear
Burley Bear & Meadow Flower

<u>Science Fiction</u>

The Savitar Series:
    Journey's End
    Savitar
    Confluence
    Savitar Collection

Bram Nielson Series
    The Fold
    The Message
    Fold Wormhole
    Negative Fold
    Ripples in Time
    Bram Nielson Collection

<u>Single Science Fiction Books</u>

    Current Past and Future
    The Event
    The Door
    Viajante 7

Ron Mueller

<u>Fiction Series</u>

The Alex Evercrest Series

The River Front
The Girl on The Grill
Missing
Maggot
Racist
Votive Candles
Windy City
Country Road
Pool of Blood
Sins of the Daughter
Body Parts
The Skull Collector
The Vanishing
The Shadow Fighter
Moonshine
Grief's Trajectory
The Magic Touch
Northern Lights
Alex Evercrest Heroin Collection
Alex Evercrest Collection Two
New Direction

A Brian Oneil Novell

Hawaiian Phoenix
Moon Curser
Death Broker
Hawaiian Princesses

The Problem Solver Series

Solutions
Drug Lords
Border Crosser
Problem Solver Collection

Imagination by Courtney Huynh and Chloe Parker

Fold Wormhole
By: *Ron Mueller*

Around the World Publishing LLC
4914 Cooper Road Suite 144
Cincinnati, Ohio 45242-9998

This story is a work of fiction. Names, characters, places, and incidents either are products of the author's imagination or are used fictitiously. Any resemblance to actual events or locales or persons, living or dead, is entirely coincidental.

Fold Wormhole, by Ron Mueller Copyright © 2023
Renewal 2024

ISBN 13: 978-1-68223-275-0
ISBN 10: 1-68223-275-1

Distributed by Ingram
Cover Picture by NASA@ShutterStock
Cover Design by: Ron Mueller

Ron Mueller

vi

Dedicated to those who will find

we can go faster

than the speed of light.

<u>Table of Content</u>

Chapter 1: Return to the Desert 1

Chapter 2: Alien Engagement 13

Chapter 3: Gaia 25

Chapter 4: Negative Space 39

Chapter 5: Political Driving Force 55

Chapter 6: Negative Fold Scouts 75

Chapter 7: Family Feud 89

Chapter 8: A Fold Vacation 101

Chapter 9: Scandinavian Food 115

Chapter 10: Highway Six 129

Chapter 11: Finland 145

Chapter 12: Oversight 161

Chapter 13: Waterworld Migration 175

Chapter 14: The Committee 189

Chapter 15: The Senator 205

Chapter 16: The Rest of the Committee 221

Chapter 17: Election 239

Chapter 18: Gabon 257

Chapter 19: A Fold in Time 269

Preview of: Negative Fold 283

About the Author 317

<u>Chapter 1 Return to the Desert</u>

The Marine guards stationed at the desert compound had been notified to clear the helo pad and then standby for an early arrival of a group of people. The guards were on their desert rotation from the Fold compound located in Dallas, Oregon so they were familiar with the Fold technology, but they had never witnessed a Fold bubble departure or arrival. It was for them one of the more exciting mornings on guard duty.

Then the bubble appeared and hovered inches off the ground. They recognized two of their own, Castor and Donna as they got out of the bubble and took up the front position. Then a very beautiful young woman emerged who they had never seen before. She was followed by another of their own, Orlando.

Then they recognized the helo pilot that periodically flew one of their gunships back at the compound.

She was followed the person they knew as the genius and his partner.

The last two that got out they knew as two of the FBI bodyguards assigned to protect the genius.

They watched as the group walked away in the dark of the morning and headed out into the desert.

The night was pitch black. Millions of stars twinkled overhead that seemed to be behind a thin white veil covering the face of heaven. Bram couldn't see his hands in front of him. He took the lead up the almost invisible path. His feet knew the way through their body memory.

The bright shimmering star light made the surrounding grasses and sage brush appear alive as the light morning breeze caused them to waver and the limited number of leaves to rustle.

He was followed by Pat, Zuri, Amy and then the rest of the protection detail.

Einstein was in his pocket.

He let everyone know that Pat, Zuri, and Amy were the only ones going to sit on the boulder that he had sat on during the development of the Fold equation. The four of them would watch the sunrise from the place where he had finally realized that he had made the breakthrough. A breakthrough that now he believed was guided by another hand.

He had thought of this outing as a way to bring Einstein for a visit to his home and to share with Zuri that instant of time that led to the miracle that she represented.

Somewhere, in one of the cracks in the boulder, was where Einstein had previously lived. Now at least five years old, Einstein would once again get to visit home.

Fold Wormhole

Bram joked that Einstein had guided him in the quest to develop the Fold equation.

When they got to the boulder, Bram helped Pat, Zuri, and Amy up and then he sat down in his usual spot. He took Einstein from his pocket and placed him down beside him.

Einstein circled around once and then disappeared down the side of the rock.

Pat asked if he would come back.

Bram said that he thought so but only when the sun broke over the horizon and its rays hit the boulder.

Zuri smiled and commented that she was honored to visit the place where Bram had sat and thought through the maze of equations that had transformed her from a very crippled person to a one with a normal body. It was, she said, a body about which she was still learning. She said that it was like a stranger returning to her home after an extreme remodeling and not recognizing most of what she saw. In her case everything about herself felt different and unknown.

Bram replied that her transformation was for him the grand reward, for his efforts here in the desert. He added it was a reward that would carry him through the rest of his life.

Pat gave Zuri a hug and said that her physical transformation was a positive reward for everyone working on the Fold project. They all believed that they had witnessed a miracle.

Amy added that she had first learned of the Fold capability sitting on the boulder and thought at the time that she had witnessed something that could never be exceeded. Then she had witnessed Zuri's transformation and knew that she had witnessed the real miracle of the Fold.

A thin bright line cut across the dark night horizon as the sun light broke over the mountains to the east and the star light seemed to wane. The line travel across the desert as if seeking the boulder. It worked its way like a thief in the night sulked up toward an open window. Its first streaks of light hit the boulder and slowly worked its way and worked upward like the thief climbing in the window. It seemed to slow as if trying to find its way, the way a mountain climber would look for hand holds as she made her way up the cliff.

Moments later Einstein came out and surprisingly another mouse followed him.

Pat commented that it seemed that Einstein had found a mate.

Bram nodded and put out two crumbs and said that he had probably lost his Fold confidant to a love affair. He said that Einstein deserved to have such an affair.

Einstein got up on his two hind legs and Bram lowered his hand. Einstein got into his palm and then the second mouse did as well. Einstein circled and lay down and the new mouse did as well.

Zuri commented that she could not believe what she was seeing.

Fold Wormhole

Bram lowered his hand and both mice got out. Einstein then led the way down to the crack from which he had come and disappeared.

Bram commented that he would return in a couple of months to see if Einstein would return to greet him.

Small bubbles, holding tea, a sweet roll, and some cherries, appeared. There was one for every person in the group.

Bram said that they should enjoy the sunrise snack that Marcus had arranged and then take a walk in the desert.

Amy got up and as she went down the boulder said that she would be picking them up in a helicopter and bringing them back for a full lunch.

Bram left his cookie crumbs on the rock and then led the way out to the desert.

He was heading out one degree from true north. That was one degree more than the last time he had made such a walk. He knew that Amy would know where to take her helo. He was silent as he thought about what seemed like only yesterday but then all of the achievements that had taken place since that time seemed to be flashing through his mind.

He felt lucky to have made the discoveries that had so far kept getting better and better and it had reached a point that he was not sure where it would take him next.

Pat quietly asked if he was OK.

Bram smiled and replied that Einstein had been a good partner in his developmental surges. He gave Pat a hug and commented that giving Einstein a hug and getting a reply from him was always a short coming and that Pat would have to step up and take up the slack.

Zuri had been walking behind them and was thinking about the wonderful relationship the two had and her heart stopped when by chance she saw the rattlesnake. She stopped and quietly said that the two soapy people walking mindlessly ahead of her should pay attention and not tangle with the rattle snake they were about to walk into.

That caused everyone to stop. Both Bram and Pat looked to where Zuri pointed with her stick to where the snake was laying in the rays of the sun. It was still lethargic from the cold of the night.

Orlando said he would take care of the snake, but Bram stopped him and commented that the snake must just have moved into the sun's rays but had not yet been able to get warmed up. He said they were on its turf and should respect its territory.

He thanked Zuri for having been alert and then led the group around the snake.

He then related the story about having walked out from a center point and having recorded the terrain at one-degree increments until he had been able to match the topography he mapped in his mind and computer to a specific location in the United States.

Fold Wormhole

He said that it had taken him a year and that today they were walking out along the three hundred and sixty first degree line.

Pat asked why the location had been so important to him.

He replied that it was a matter of principle. He was angry that sufficient security could be provided to so many important people, but he had to be treated like a criminal who was sent into isolated confinement. He was sure that it had to do with the fact that the folks had decided his ideas would be extremely powerful and they had wanted to ensure that the power it represented would not leak out of the country.

He pointed out that the leaks so far had come not from those associated most closely to the Fold project but from the very people worried about the leaks.

Zuri asked what he had done when he finally determined the location.

He replied that he had confronted Jeffrey and Erica and threatened to leak the desert location to the media. He made the point that the confrontation with the two was the beginning of the change that led to the social environment that they were now living in at the Fold compound.

He highlighted the fact that the confrontation had changed his relationship with Erica and subsequently changed her life.

Up until that time Erica wanted to be in control and thought that he wanted her role. She was upset because Jeffrey had given him the best apartment to live in. She believed that she was not being respected.

Pat commented that she had talked to Erica before coming back to the desert and had learned that for Erica the return to the desert would have been a return to a time that she now considered a dark time that she had successfully escaped and that she preferred leaving it in the desert.

Bram nodded and said that Erica was now living a different life with a new set of values and had found her soul mate and would most likely be happy for the rest of her life.

They had been walking for almost two hours when Zuri commented that she could not see the helicopter, but she heard it.

Bram pointed to a dark spot that seemed to be just above the ground that was fast approaching from the center point that was the compound buildings.

He commented that Amy had always flown her helicopter awfully close to the ground so she could pick him out as she passed over him.

He shared the fact that when he had some sort of place to hide he would do so on her first pass and then continue walking and wait until she realized that she had missed him and returned to pick him up.

It was a game of cat and mouse between the two of them the whole time they had been in the desert.

Pat shared that Amy had shared the fact that she knew that the two of them were always playing a cat and mouse game that she had learned to enjoy. It was, she said always the most fun part of her day.

Fold Wormhole

Bram smiled and said that it was also a great way for him to start each day and that game had earned Amy the privilege of being the first person with whom he had shared the Fold breakthrough. He had taken her to the boulder and there he had introduced Einstein to her, and they had the same breakfast snack that they had just shared earlier.

Zuri commented that Bram had a desert experience that became the fabric that was still guiding the Fold program and one that she now personally embraced.

Bram smiled and commented that it was a very positive influence in his life and that the fabric of that life had been woven by his mother when as a young boy, she repeatedly told him that he had to treat others the way he wished to be treated. She had also said that if he embraced that one saying, his life would be rich whether he was a pauper, a wise man, or a genius.

He added that he tried to practice that philosophy even when he had the urge to kick some people in their derriere.

Pat laughed and said that most people would just say that they had the urge to kick some people in their butt.

Zuri asked what word she should use when she attended Oxford University.

Pat said that she thought Bum or arse depending on the social situation.

Bram laughed and said that they should get into the hilo and enjoy the ride back to the compound.

Amy landed her hilo in an open area and waved them onboard. She had Zuri sit in the front seat. Once everyone was in and had their safety harness on, she handed them each headsets.

They all got in and watched as Orlando led the rest of the group on foot back toward the compound. He had them singing a ditty and led off at a good jog.

Bram then told Zuri that she was about to experience a hair-raising flight that he had to endure every morning before working on the Fold equation and that she would learn why he finally had to make a breakthrough. He said that Amy had frightened him into being successful.

Amy laughed and then took off and flew out away from the desert compound. She flew just above the surface at a dizzying speed. She had arranged with Orlando to fly out long enough to let him get back to the compound.

Zuri shouted that she did want to live to enjoy going to Oxford.

Bram laughed and said that Amy would make sure that Zuri was so afraid to fail that she would graduate at the top of her class.

Amy took a sharp bank and headed back to the compound. She did a little up bob and then set the helo down at the center of the landing pad.

She looked over at Zuri and asked if she had enjoyed the ride.

Fold Wormhole

Zuri nodded and said it had been much, much more exciting than the Wheel One flight to the back of the moon.

Bram added that the flight in from the desert had always been exciting for him and that he had made sure that Amy went to astronaut training in an attempt to train her to be a normal pilot. He now realized that it had not worked.

Amy said that flying a helo had been and still was one of the most enjoyable things that she did. She said that she had convinced the Marines back at the compound to let her fly one of their gunships on a regular basis. It had allowed her to keep up her flying skill during her time back at the Fold compound.

Bram said he would now worry about who was flying the protection helo when he jogged into work in the mornings.

Pat said that she had just thought of a good ditty for their next jog in

> *Who's that flying in the sky?*
> *Who's that flying way down so low.*
> *Is that someone that we know?*
> *If its Amy then it's so.*
> *Who's that flying in the sky*
> *Is that someone that we know?*
> *Yo, Ho, Yo, Ho*
> *Look how low, Look how low.*
> *Fly crazy, Ho, Ho, Ho.*

Bram pointed to Orlando, Castor and Donna who were standing with Zoe and Eric at the side of the helo landing area. He commented that they had made good time getting back and he was sure that they would all have a great lunch before heading back to the Dallas Fold compound.

The return to the Fold compound via bubble was scheduled after their lunch.

Chapter 2: Alien Engagement

Sunday morning Bram rode the two-person elevator to his basement office. He made himself a cup of pour through coffee and sat down at his computer. He worked his entire equation with negative time to see if it would give him an insight to what might happen. What he learned was that his equation using negative time seemed to go in a circle or at least it became nonlinear and perhaps be a spiral. It seemed to defy definition or relation to one particular shape.

Pat, Zoe, and Eric came in and said they had been worried about where he had gone and that he had broken the protection protocol.

He nodded and said that it had never registered when he got on the elevator to come down to his office. He suggested they put in a camera and alarm so that when he did it again, they would immediately know.

Pat reminded him that they had agreed to go to the neighborhood recreation center for lunch where Melisa had gathered some of the younger children who they were going to play various games with.

Bram knew that his time thinking about negative space was over for the day.

He woke up on Monday ready to attack the day. On their five thirty in the morning jog into work, Castor took up the ditty that Pat had shared when they had gotten off the helo in the desert.

> *Who's that flying in the sky?*
> *Who's that flying way down so low.*
> *Is that someone that we know?*
> *If its Amy then it's so.*
> *Who's that flying in the sky*
> *Is that someone that we know?*
> *Yo, Ho, Yo, Ho*
> *Look how low, Look how low.*
> *Fly crazy, Ho, Ho, Ho.*

Both he and Donna pointed to the helo overhead and Bram watched as it came down low to one side and wiggled and then went back up. He had not been able to see the pilot but figured it was Amy.

At that moment he was thinking about the response he was waiting for from the Aliens. It had been sent to them the day after Christmas. He figured that it would take them time to react to the message. The few days had passed, and he hoped a reply had been returned.

Fold Wormhole

He, Marcus and Mallica were scheduled to check the location where they had originally intercepted the Alien's first message to see if a reply had been sent back.

Linda welcomed him back and reminded him about his meeting and asked about the rest of his day and when he wanted to update his two-week calendar.

Bram suggested that updating the calendar should take place in the late afternoon. He asked that she set up a meeting with Remi and check with Jose to see when he could take possession of the first giant bubble.

He then asked to get a meeting set up with Erica to discuss the building of another bubble and to check on any other financial issues.

Linda gave a small laugh and asked if this was just today's items or was it the two-week items.

Bram said he would be in his office to start the day and then he would meet with Marcus and Mallica.

Bob and Thomas took their chairs as Bram pressed the heat lever on the water pot.

Bram sat down at his desk and put his hand at the center of the Milky Way Spiral picture that was under the glass on his desk. He was thinking about the Wormhole equation and the negative space aspect of the reversing process. He was anxious to investigate what going into negative space would mean.

He fired up his laptop and reviewed the equation yet again. He had it burned into his mind and really did not need to see it but doing so let him imagine what might happen. It was like having a book in his hand that allowed him to feel the weight of the story. He was trying to envision the resulting shape of his negative equation.

Linda's call that he had ten minutes before his scheduled meeting with Marcus and Mallica brought him out of his speculation about the negative part of space. He realized that he had spent almost an hour deep in thought and that he had not made the tea that he had intended to make.

He looked over at Bob and Thomas and realized that the two of them had used the hot water to make themselves tea and had made him a cup as well, but it was still sitting at the refreshment center.

Unlike Zoe that was willing to pull him up from the depth, these two were not willing to take that chance.

He smiled and thanked them for the tea and said that it was time for them to go with him to his next meeting.

Marcus and Mallica were waiting outside of his office and suggested they go to the lab where the bubble that had been sent out to see if the Aliens had responded, had just been returned to its holding area. They had arranged for Remi to retrieve the computer recording. He had volunteered to review it on his computer.

Fold Wormhole

Bram thanked them for getting everything ready. He hoped that there would be a response.

Remi greeted them and said that there was something on the computer, but he had resisted getting into it until they all arrived. He pointed to a large screen and said he would now open the folder with the message.

When the message came on the screen, Bram had an immediate smile on his face. The first line was in English, "Greetings, we on Swoosh are elated that intelligent beings have received our message and were able to respond to us using our language. We are extremely impressed. To be offered aid dried our eyes and caused us to surface and breach."

Then the messaged changed to the alien language and provided more information about themselves, their population numbers, and the number of species in their world. There was an explanation that they did not have physical structures as had been described existing on Earth. They were amazed that the human species lived on land and breathed air directly.

They added that the energy required to send the reply had exhausted their energy resource and it would take at least another journey around their star to rejuvenate it.

They then gave some data about the condition of their star.

Mallica commented the lack of power, and any significant structures had signaled her that rescuing the Aliens and transporting them to another water world had just gotten more complicated.

Marcus wondered how a species that could think deeply and develop a Fold message transmitter would not have developed the ability to build a large energy source.

On Earth, electricity, gas engines, and steam engines all existed in abundance. Often the power source had preceded the use it was eventually used for. He said it was hard for him to understand how the technology to send out the Fold message had been developed.

Bram agreed that it seemed inconceivable, but reality said that it had been done. He speculated about the whales and the dolphins and wondered if on Earth they had superior thoughts but were not able to develop the technology to communicate with humans.

Mallica then brought them back and asked about the response and pointed out that Earth would have to supply the short-term capability for the Aliens on Swoosh to begin to make the move to another water world.

Bram agreed. He pointed out that the first transport that would hold two maybe three of the Swooshians was ready for delivery. The three of them had to agree on the delivery coordinates and then make the Fold from the hangar in Seattle to the coordinate.

Marcus suggested a coordinate near the Alien water world that they had previously used since it would save time since he would not need to verify the spot did not have a field of debris.

Fold Wormhole

Bram agreed and let Marcus know that the Fold would happen that afternoon. He had a meeting with Erica with the objective of her ordering a second bubble. He asked Marcus to call Jose at the building site to verify the coordinate of the bubbles center.

Then they would meet at three and Fold the bubble out to the coordinate near Swoosh.

Mallica asked whether they would respond to the reply from Swoosh.

Bram suggested that she get a message ready that asked the Aliens for the current chemistry on Swoosh and how soon the Swooshians would be ready to check out the new water worlds that met the parameters that were agreed on.

Mallica suggested they also ask how quickly the Swooshians were planning to make the transition to a new world.

Bram agreed and added that with the current Fold capacity it would take more than their lifetime to get just a small percentage of Swooshians to a new planet. He said they would need to figure out a way to set up a transport system that had higher capacity and one that did not rely on the Earth for the materials or the manufacturing of the bubbles.

He asked if she and Marcus might take that on as a project. They could recruit other folks, like Remi or anyone else that could add the knowledge they needed to set up a remote bubble production system.

Mallica said that a project like that would be exciting for her. She said that she was up for it and would get a group together to flesh out who needed to be on the team.

Bram thanked her and said that Marcus already had his hands full with determining where bubbles should Fold and making sure the Fold location was clear of debris. He expected that Marcus would be extremely critical in determining the coordinates for a bubble factory.

Marcus agreed and said he was excited about suggesting locations within the Swooshian solar system that might position the production facility near the materials needed to make the giant bubbles.

He then added that perhaps some even better locations would be in some other solar system near a planet that had the materials critical in making the bubbles.

He said that once he was given the ingredients from which the bubbles were made, the files with the data from the previously discovered planets could be examined and an optimum location could be selected. Perhaps the facility could be on the surface of such a planet but at a minimum it could be nearby, and materials mined and sent out to the production facility.

Bram said he had heard enough, and he was going back to his office and begin to work on his next project.

Fold Wormhole

He was walking back to his office thinking about the negative realm of his equation when Erica intercepted him near the cafeteria.

She asked if Bram knew that it was lunch time.

He shook his head and said that it seemed that the time was flying.

Erica suggested that he follow her, and they would meet up with Pat for lunch.

Bram followed her into the cafeteria and waved at Pat who was sitting by herself at their usual table.

Erica had selected an Italian salad and was almost immediately on the way to the table.

Bram was not sure what he wanted. He looked over the offering and went for a slice of beef, asparagus, and a small, baked potato. He carried his tray out to the table and then decided that he wanted a lemonade to go with what he had selected.

Pat asked how his day was progressing.

Bram commented that he seemed to be constantly behind in what he had been planning to get accomplished.

Erica waited until Bram had finished and was sipping his lemonade and then asked him what their meeting was about and could they have it now.

Bram smiled and said that it was a short topic. He was having the current bubble moved out of the hangar in the afternoon and he was interested in getting another one on order.

Erica nodded, made a note on her phone, and then said it was done. She then said the order would be in by the end of day.

Bram thanked her and said that her meeting was one that had happened quickly and ahead of time. He said that when he got back into the office he would be able to focus on his next project.

He was leaving the cafeteria when he decided that where he needed to go was to the Lab and see if a bubble was available that he could use. His turn toward the Lab caught Castor and Donna by surprise and they hustled to get back in the lead and then asked where he was going.

Bram apologized and said that he had decided to see if a bubble that he could use was available.

Remi had left the cafeteria on Bram's heal and overheard the exchange. He said that he had several bubbles ready, but they would need the Fold coordinate programed in.

Bram replied that he was going to use the Neptune coordinates and that once they were programed in he was going out to try an experiment.

Remi asked about the experiment.

Bram shared that he was going to nibble at the impact that negative time had on the Fold reverse equation.

Remi asked why he did not send out the bubble on its own.

Bram said that he had done that previously and that there was nothing recorded on the visual or the coordinate calculator.

Remi shook his head and asked if there was a way to hook up a second bubble that could pull him back.

Fold Wormhole

Bram said that he did not know how to program such a bubble and said that he felt that once he had a personal experience, he would be able to figure out how to navigate the negative space region.

Remi then suggested waiting until morning so that Bram would have an entire day.

Bram thought about it and said that the suggestion made sense, and they should plan to use the next day to do the initial exploration of the negative Fold space.

He spent the rest of the afternoon deciding what he wanted to learn in the negative Fold space.

That afternoon as they were riding back to the house, when Pat asked what he was planning for the next day, Bram shared that he was planning to venture into the negative Fold space.

He was surprised by the silence that followed.

He asked why there was no reaction.

Pat replied that she was thinking through what was bothering her and she would share her thoughts after dinner.

Bram found it hard to wait. Finally, after dinner he led the way down into his office and sat down on the two-person recliner. He was pleased that Pat sat down next to him and said that she was ready to share her concern and to ask him to do several things when he ventured into the negative Fold area.

She said that she was afraid that the scientific laws that were more or less absolute in their current reality would not hold in the negative Fold reality. She then asked how he thought time and space would function in the negative reality.

Bram admitted that he was not sure about anything in the negative Fold reality.

Pat asked whether he would consider waiting before Folding into the Negative.

Bram replied that he had considered that but there were no additional actions or developments that he could envision so he was planning to make the negative Fold to see if he could personally learn what was going on.

Pat then said that she wanted him to take enough food and water for a week with him.

She asked if he could use his body to gauge time. Or was there a way for him to separately keep track of time other than his computer.

She had no idea how he would be able to gauge distance and asked if he had an idea.

Bram thanked her for the food and time ideas and admitted that he was relatively clueless about everything that he might encounter.

He mentioned that her questions had triggered several ideas that he would act on in the morning.

<u>Chapter 3: Gaia</u>

The next morning on the jog in, Zoe was the one that led them through a ditty.

> *Negative Fold*
> *Negative Fold*
> *Hold the phone.*
> *Bram is clueless.*
> *Loose screw to us*
> *Clueless, Clueless*
> *Negative Fold*
> *Hold, Hold*
> *Stop the Fold*
> *Don't be foolish.*
> *Don't be bold.*
> *Negative Fold*
> *Negative Fold*

The entire compound resounded with the echo as the other Marines joining in.

Linda greeted him and commented that it seemed that the morning ditty might be a warning to which he should listen. She reminded him that this was the day that had been agreed on to Fold to the Swooshian world and that he would need to delay his negative Fold until the following day.

Bram thanked Linda for reminding him and agreed to do the negative Fold the next day. He asked her to work with Pat and arrange for a cooler of food to be added to the bubble that was being prepared for the negative fold.

Remi showed Bram a much larger bubble that had been modified to include a small latrine and a bed to sleep on.

When Bram asked about the modifications, Remi responded that Pat had made the request and he thought it had been from him, but he thought it was a great idea, so he made the modifications.

Bram said that the modifications were a good idea.

He then asked if Remi would come up with a common mechanical clock that could be digitized and add that to the modifications he was making.

Bram went to the printer and grabbed a good supply of paper, and he grabbed a mechanical pencil, a French curve, and a square from the drawing table.

He was now thinking through what his survival strategy should be. This had all been triggered by Pat and her concern.

He found the sensor that would sense the second hand on the mechanical clock and interfaced it with the computer program that was keeping track of time. He wanted to ensure that the time controlling his computer was the time that was flowing in the left to right direction.

Fold Wormhole

He wanted it to be distinctly his time not the negative Fold time and he felt the mechanical clock was a technology that was more resistant to negative time.

He then asked if the other bubbles that would go to the Alien planet of Swoosh were ready and if everyone on the list had checked in.

Remi assured him that the bubbles and everyone was ready for their noon launch. He commented that Marcus had estimated that their arrival would be sometime in the morning hours on Swoosh.

Bram smiled and said that he hoped that the Swooshians had the same wake-sleep cycle that humans had.

Gerry had been working on populating his team with a mix of experts. He had focused on the environmental and chemistry specialists. He wanted to be able to verify the suitability of the water worlds that had been identified as the potential new homes for the Swooshians.

He had also familiarized himself with the lab sampling bubbles that were to be used for the detailed analysis of the environment of each of the worlds. He was impressed with the capabilities and the equipment of the labs.

He wondered where Bram was getting the funding to cover the cost of the various projects that were underway. He had asked that of Erica and had been told that the money pipeline would remain full at least while the current President was in office.

He was pleased with each of the six members on the team. The analysts would stay at the compound. The team would take turns Folding to the water worlds.

He had a meeting with Bram to finalize the Folds to the four water worlds he and his team would analyze.

He had started to think of Bram as the Five Star Admiral of the Fold program. He would have to tell Admiral Becker, his sponsor that he had found that Five Star Admiral that they had always joked about.

Bram greeted Gerry and asked if he had been able to get his team organized and ready to go into action.

Gerry replied that he was impressed with the capabilities and the eagerness of all the applicants. He said he had focused on seeing how they got along with himself and with each other before making the final selection decision.

Bram said that he had worked hard at making sure any person that came onto the Fold team had the capability and had an inclusive attitude.

Gerry complimented Bram on being successful in his recruiting and that Erica had adopted the same approach.

He then noted that to date the Fold retention record stood at an unheard of one hundred percent.

Bram smiled and said that he figured it was the pool parties and the great food that was having that effect.

Fold Wormhole

Gerry shared that all of the equipment in the four labs had been tested, the bubbles had been prepared and everything was a go.

Bram thanked him for being ready and that the noon departure was still on.

The Fold to the Swoosh system happened at noon sharp. The two bubbles Folded to the coordinates that Marcus had researched and had worked with Remi to make sure it was a clear location and that it would be near the planet so that they could get a water and atmosphere sample.

Bram asked Mallica to make first contact with the Swooshians.

She asked if he was sure that he didn't want to be first.

Bram smiled and said that her Swooshian accent was better than his or at least they would soon find out. He pointed out that she was by far the best at understanding the Swooshian language.

She got on the Fold transmitter and sent a message of greeting to the planet. She was not sure how to aim her transmission.

Bram had suggested that they hit the surface of the planet from pole to pole as it rotated so that it would not matter where it might be received. The first part of the message should clearly give the coordinate of their bubble so they could learn where the message was being received.

There was a delay of a response but then the Swooshians responded with a greeting that spoke of their amazement at the ability for their Earthling friends to be able to make the journey to their star system.

Bram then suggested they launch their underwater transmitter so they could speak to the Swooshians using a radio transmitter.

Mallica checked with the Swooshian she was in contact with and received an OK to the underwater transmitter. It was both a transmitter and it was capable of sending back a signal to the bubbles. Once it was in place Mallica tried out her skill at speaking Swooshian.

Bram was pleased with the response that they received that complemented Mallica at sounding very much like a Swooshian from the southern hemisphere.

He then asked in Swooshian what part of Swoosh he might be from.

He smiled when the reply said that his accent was a local one.

Pat then asked if they could take samples of the waters and the atmosphere so they could compare it to the waters and the atmosphere of the potential planets that had been found for the Swooshian population.

Bram smiled when the reply was that of course they could take the samples, and the question was if an exploratory Swooshian team might be able to learn more about the planets that had been discovered.

Fold Wormhole

He shared the fact that a special analysis team was set up to analyze the Swooshian samples and then see if the samples from the other planets were within tolerance. Once a match was made, he suggested that the Swooshian explorers should take a trip to the planets and determine which would be the most desirable.

He asked if there was any concern that the bubble that would be their transport would only hold three Swooshians.

The Swooshian responded that they were amazed that a vessel large enough to hold three of them was available. They asked how the materials and the power to Fold such mass was available.

Bram replied that the exploratory Fold energy would be provided by an Earth energy relay feed, but that future Folds would need to utilize the energy of the Swooshian star. And materials to make more transport bubbles would need to be mined locally from the planets that were part of the Swooshian system.

The Swooshian that Bram was conversing with commented that those that were with him were amazed with the speed of response that they had received, and they were overwhelmed with the ease at which their new Earth friends spoke of mining the materials from planets in their star system.

They had been concerned about sending out a call for help in fear of finding unfriendly aliens that might take advantage of the Swooshian world.

Now they were ready to breach the surface in leaps of joy.

Bram replied that when they learned the violent history of Earth, fear would once again be part of their thinking.

He let them know that he was acting on his own to ensure that the Swooshian world would have its own capability to save themselves and would not be relying on Earth to make it happen.

The Earth society currently was ignorant of the technology that would save the Swoshians and when technology became known, Earth would experience a great upheaval.

Pat came on and said that the samples had been taken and the sample bubbles were now being analyzed.

Bram asked Marcus to share what would be the next steps to getting the Swooshians capable of being transported to the bubbles.

Marcus asked for specific coordinates where each Swooshian would be located, and he wanted the size and the weight of each Swooshian. He explained that when the time came these individuals would be Folded into the transport bubble and then the bubble would be Folded to the planet that they would explore.

He said that he would return in the near future to facilitate the Fold of Swooshians to the exploration bubble and that at that time the information he was asking for would need to be exact.

Bram shared that he expected that everything to make the Swooshians capable to explore their new world would be put in place.

He then gave the coordinates of the relay bubble where the Swooshians should send their messages and from where Earth would send their reply.

Mallica thanked the Swooshians for their welcome and said that she hoped that in the near future Earth would be ready to host them.

Bram then closed by wishing them all good swimming and that he looked forward to their next meeting.

On their return Lacy met them and asked to speak to Bram in private.

Bram was curious about what Lacy might have to share with him. She had been very effective in eliminating the physical attacks and had set up a surveillance system that provided another level of protection.

He was surprised at the topic that came up.

Lacy came in and said that she had learned that there was a bill in the Senate to put a watch dog committee in an overview and approval position of what was being done at the Fold facility.

Bram asked how long before that bill came to a vote and if there was any way to delay or defeat it.

Lacy said that she had contacted Jeffrey and asked him to see if he could delay it for as long as possible. It was not a question of defeating it because there are supporters on both sides of the aisle.

Bram asked Lacy to keep on top of it and to let him know how soon such a committee could be formed and put in place.

He had already decided to move the entire Fold operation to another location. A location that would be impossible for the committee to exercise oversight control. It would be on another world and in another star system.

He knew that time was the constraint in being able to make such a move.

Once Lacy left, Bram asked that Linda set up an immediate meeting with Erica and one with Marcus.

Erica went to Bram's office and wondered what he might want. She was thinking about his return from Swoosh and the meeting with the Swooshians and was anticipating something associated with the Fold.

Bram greeted Erica and brought her up to date with what was going on in the Senate.

He then asked her how quickly she could have prefabricated structures set up on the clear empty compound area. He wanted to build a small, prefabricated city with a dozen homes and several warehouses. He said that she should think of a miniature Fold community and get it all built.

He went on to also request a computer center and a multidisciplinary lab.

Erica smiled and asked if she had a week or a month to do what he was requesting.

Bram said that he was not sure but that she should talk to Lacy to get a feel for the timing. He was going to Fold all the structures to a location that only he would know.

Lacy smiled and said that he was becoming a real rebel, and she was pleased to be on his team. She said that when the time came, he should be sure to take her along.

Bram said that he would of course make sure she was on the list, but he was not sure of the timing.

As Lacy left the office, Marcus and Remi were waiting to enter. Lacy commented that they were about to get a surprise.

The two entered and Marcus asked what was up.

Bram updated them and shared what his plans were.

Remi gave a grunt and said that having an oversight committee would stall all their work and that moving the work to another location was indeed the answer but a challenging and time consuming one.

Bram asked Remi if he was willing to lead the analysis of the four Earth-like worlds that Marcus had found.

Remi said that he was honored to be asked and that he would send out sampling bubbles to each that day and have them analyzed by the end of the following day.

Bram looked at Marcus and said that as the prefab buildings got set up he would like to get them Folded to the world that he and Remi agreed was the most suitable. He asked that he and Marcus find the most suitable location to set up such a city.

Marcus asked what they would call the selected world.

Bram suggested Gaia.

Marcus replied that he liked the idea of using an ancient Greek deity as the source of the name.

Bram said that he was sure that Pat or someone else would want to have a naming contest. He said he was fine with another name as well. More important to him than the name was that it would be available for them to utilize on a time frame that made sense.

He asked the two of them to work with Pat and Amy in determining the layout for the new city they were about to establish.

He shared that not all the folks in the current organization would be able to be relocated to the new world and that they should think about if they personally wanted to relocate.

Marcus thanked him and said that he would discuss this at home. He was not sure how Myla would react. He said that Myla had been doing well in her recovery from the abuse she had suffered when she was a young girl, but he was not sure how she would take to the idea of moving to another world.

Remi commented that he was certain he would like to go but that he would be open to initially staying put.

Bram said that they would get together later to develop a transition plan. He personally would most likely be living in both worlds. He would need to keep up the appearance that the current site was fully functional.

Linda buzzed in and gave him his end of the day ten-minute warning.

Fold Wormhole

Bram walked out to the van that would transport him home. He looked at the armored truck that had the lead position, his van that was in the middle and the armored truck that was behind it. He marveled at the small army of guards that protected his movement inside of a fenced in and guarded compound.

Bob commented that his job would keep him on guard duty as long as Bram was thought to be on Earth but when the time came he would like to be considered for the opportunity to go to another world.

Thomas said that he was with Bob on the request.

Bram replied that he would keep the request in mind, but he would not make any promises until the actual time came to make a choice.

He smiled and said that the choice might come much sooner than anyone might imagine.

On the way home Pat listened as Bram brought her up to speed on what had transpired. She asked how Bram planned to get a small city built on another world in time to avoid the oversight committee.

Bram replied that he was hoping that she would become a city planner and builder.

Pat replied that she would be glad to get involved and lead such an effort, but it would require folks that were real city planners. She said she was sure that Amy would also love to be involved. They had both talked about the fact that being called

Captain no longer held much allure or meaning and they were both ready to sink their teeth into some meaningful project.

Bram suggested that she contact Erica who would be able to get the right resources. He said that Erica was onboard with his desire to establish this small city on another world.

Chapter 4: Negative Space

Bram had been pulled away from his exercise with the Fold equation to stay involved with communicating with the Swoshians now he was eager to get back to learning about the negative Fold space realm. On his arrival at the office, he asked Linda to have the cafeteria fill the order that Pat had given Chef D'Carluca for a weeks' worth of meals. He joked with her and said that the two of them could go on a picnic when he returned in the afternoon.

Linda replied that she felt like putting in more food so he would not go hungry and if he did return in the afternoon, she would invited extra people to the picnic.

Bram thanked her for her lack of confidence and said he was heading out to meet Remi and go over the bubble interior to make sure everything was ready.

Linda waited until Bram had left and then called in an additional cooler to be loaded with sandwiches and other items that kept well.

When he entered the Lab, everything went silent. Bram had gotten used to the reaction of the lab folks but this time the bustle did not restart. He took this as the fact that they all thought he was about to take a risk about which they were concerned.

He had sent out three scout bubbles that had never returned so he was concerned as well, but he figured that once he understood the problem with what happened to the three bubbles that had not returned, he would be able to solve the return problem.

He knew that Pat was super worried because she had not said a word about his Fold into the negative space since their discussion the evening before.

Chef D'Carluca arrived to personally deliver three coolers and to stock up the small refrigerator that Remi had installed in the bubble. He said nothing about the extra food that Linda had added or the same amount of food that he had added. He had also filled Pat's food order.

He figured that Bram had at least three weeks of food in the three coolers he put into the bubble.

Bram knew that the bubble was the largest that Remi had so far constructed, yet it seemed like a tight fit.

Remi explained that he had added extra battery power so that Bram could sparingly heat the interior. Remi then opened a locker and pointed to a space suit that had its own oxygen feed. He made the point that if the bubble was breached Bram should immediately get into his suit that would give him almost a days' worth of time.

Fold Wormhole

Bram then knew that Remi was as worried as everyone else.

Marcus arrived and made sure that Bram had the most up to date coordinates of all of the solar systems they had so far explored and put others in as well. He said he had included the coordinates of every new world that they had found including Swoosh.

Bram hoped that all the worries being displayed would all be for naught. The overwhelming concern was having an effect on him, and he decided that it was time to Fold to his first negative coordinate.

He felt that this first negative coordinate which was for only a few centimeters would allow him to recover and backtrack if he felt that things had gone wrong.

Pat gave him a hug and in an unusual display she gave him a long kiss. She whispered that she had his back and that she would make sure he came back.

Bram thanked her and had to turn and enter the bubble so she would not see the tears that she had generated.

Bram took his seat and waved to all the folks that he knew would be watching. He smiled and said that they should talk to Linda about the picnic they would have when he returned.

He then pressed the button that triggered the first negative Fold.

The black void of space with countless stars appeared as streaks of light that made the screens look like a fourth of July starburst explosion display.

Bram knew immediately that negative space did not act in any way similar to the positive space in which his world existed.

The streaks of light stopped, and Bram knew that he was at the initial coordinates that he had programmed. He just had no idea where he was.

The area around him was an empty portion of space. Bram knew that the path of the solar system was along a spiral at the edge of the Milky way galaxy. The time to make one rotation was close to two hundred and twenty million years. So, the only logical thing that he could conclude was that time and distance did not stay synchronized as it did in positive space. He knew immediately that his problem was a significant one. If they indeed acted independently and he did not know how to manipulate time as he did distance, he was lost. It was like being dropped into an unknown forest in an unknown country on an unknown continent.

He knew he was in big trouble.

He felt that the initial miniscule distance he had programed should have him close to his own solar system.

He used his on-board telescope that was hooked to the screen and saw what looked like a solar system at the farthest distance that it reached. He figured out the coordinates and then entered them into the computer and pressed the Fold button.

The stars once again appeared to be streaks of light and then the bubble stopped.

Fold Wormhole

Bram was out at the edge of the solar system. He noted that if it was the star that was his Sun then he must have traveled back in time. There were two planets that clearly were covered in water. One was in the position that Earth would orbit, and the other was in the position that Mars would orbit.

He determined the coordinate that would place him within the radius of the moon. It was then he noticed that there was no Moon!

He was then sure that it was a very young Earth, and it seemed to have more water than the Earth that was his home. He took note that there was only one huge continent surrounded by water. He could not see any living thing that was on a very wet continent that was barely above the water.

He determined the coordinate for the planet that he was sure was Mars. When he came out of his Fold, he was looking down at a world that was also covered in water. It, however, seemed to have plants or something green in the waters that were undulating as if dancing to a slow love musical of the sixties or a sad melody of one of the spaghetti westerns.

It was clear to Bram that life had first appeared on Mars. He wondered what happened that caused the planet to lose its water and become the bone-dry planet of his time.

Bram took a few moments to estimate where in time he might be. After a few moments of thinking about it he estimated that he was several billion years in the past.

He wondered how he would be able to return to his own time. He was certain that it would not be a linear path back and at the moment he was clueless on how to determine how to manipulate time.

Hunger interrupted his train of thought.

He looked at his mechanical clock and realized it had been more than twenty-four hours since he had folded, and he had so far not eaten or had any sleep. He decided to have a sandwich and then try out the bed that was on the other side of the latrine.

He realized he had a major problem, and it was one that at the moment he had no clue how to solve. In fact, he realized that he did not understand what the problem was.

He took a wet towel bath as Pat had suggested. He realized that she had put in all the items that allowed him to take it. Afterwards he felt refreshed and ready to sleep.

When he awoke he checked to see if he was still at the coordinates at which he had stopped. He was surprised to find that he was not. This was something that he had not anticipated.

He checked to see how long he had slept and realized that he had been out for more than twelve hours. In that internal passage of time the exterior time in negative space must have changed much more dramatically.

He was no longer in the solar system!

He had no idea of the Bubbles coordinates.

Fold Wormhole

He decided to try the coordinates to the first of four Earth like worlds he planned to visit. He wanted to visit each as quickly as possible and then visit the water worlds and end up at Swoosh as soon as possible.

He was hoping to get to a location that allowed him to Fold near to an Earth that was within a time that he would recognize.

Three Folds later with no signs of getting to the locations he had hoped, he was ready to try the Swoosh coordinates. The visit attempts to each of the previous worlds seemed to have happened at random times that he felt could be millions of or billions of years before the current Earth time.

He continued to feel ignorant of how time presented itself.

He realized that the realm of negative Fold had no linearity of time associated with it. Instead, it was more like a negative rhombicosidodecahedron (RCDH) with time randomly leaping from the edge of the negative time sphere to some other point on the spheres edge.

He knew that it would take him a significant amount of time and many experiments to see if he could learn to control movement in the negative Fold realm.

Time was a precious resource that he knew he was running out of as he ate yet another sandwich from the diminishing supply in the coolers. He had come to realize that Linda had indeed added more food to Pat's order. It seemed that everyone had added something that they thought he might need. He realized that he had many people worried about him.

He decided he needed to begin rationing his food so that he would not starve to death.

He put in the Fold coordinates for Swoosh.

He realized these coordinates were closer in time than previous coordinates because Swooshes Star was into its early death throes. He had no clue how far from the actual time he was off. He decided to experiment with trying different Folds that were close to the one where he was.

After about a dozen such attempts and at least two of his normal Earth days he realized that he still had no clue how to find the right coordinates on his imaginary RCDH Archimedean sphere with more than sixty-two regular points on its surface. In fact, it might have thousands if the Folds were going to sub points of that surface.

He realized how totally lost he was and that getting back to Earth was going to take a miracle.

He decided to get another good night's sleep. When he woke up, he again tried to figure out how to get back to his time.

In the "morning" he found himself looking out at the Swooshian Star, but he knew immediately that he had gone farther back in time because the sun was in a state of good health.

He wrestled with the coordinate thinking about how to do so on the surface of a sphere where each segment represented a different time. After three Folds he learned to increment closer to the current Earth time.

Fold Wormhole

However, the sphere he seemed to be in currently encompassed the Swooshian system. It did not include the Earth, and he had no idea how to set the coordinates for the surface of the rhombicosidodecahedron surface that would encompass the Earth in the negative universe.

He was about to throw up his hands when the clicking on his radio receiver registered in his mind that it was morse code. He figured the only way for it to be possible was that it was being sent out via the Fold transmitter that he and Remi had just developed and it was the message that Remi had first sent out, "the quick brown fox jumped over the lazy dogs back." And then it was followed with a morse code in Swooshian that said, "follow the light, follow the blinking light, and at the very end it spelled out, I have your back, follow the blinking light."

Bram used the scope and at the extreme edge of the scope's range he saw the blinking light. He set the coordinates that he could determine that would get him closer to the blinking light.

The message coming in got stronger, but it took him another four Folds before the light became steady and then each subsequent Fold got him closer to the source. He realized that he had taken more than a dozen Folds before he felt that he was back to his own time.

But a scene from one of the movies that had a fighter pilot calling in as he approached a landing on an aircraft carrier that he was coming in hot was really appropriated. He was coming in blind and hot. He had no clue how to land his bubble.

He hoped the source was a few feet above the surface and approximately at the center of the bubble he was in.

He took out the last sandwich and took a bite and then hit the Fold button. He had hoped it would be his last Fold, but it took him three more times and he was chewing on the last bite of his last sandwich when the inside of the Hanger surrounded his bubble.

He then received instructions to put the coordinates that had just been sent to him into his computer and then do one more Fold. He recognized the determined voice Pat used when she was doing something she felt strongly about. It was not a request but an order that any Marine General would have followed.

He watched as the area around the bubble became surrounded by what seemed to be the entire Fold organization.

He was almost knocked over as Pat ran to him and jumped into his arms.

She asked him if he knew how long he had been gone.

Bram replied that he could only estimate that it had been much longer than he had anticipated and that even by rationing the food he had eaten it all.

Pat had tears in her eyes as she informed him that he had been gone for more than a month. Everyone had been concerned about him running out of food, but it seems that everyone had added extra out of concern.

Fold Wormhole

Bram waved at everyone and said that they should plan to attend a celebration that Linda would arrange with all the extra food that he had come back with.

Linda laughed and asked if there was any food at all in the bubble.

Bram shook his head and said that he had eaten his last bite and had sipped his last bit of fluid which was a beer that he had found in the fridge.

He then asked how Pat had come up with a way to reach him. She said that it had been an idea that, Remi, Marcus, Mallica and she had come up with. Remi had suggested using morse code, she asked about sending out light via the Fold message magnetron, Marcus had provided more than a thousand coordinates of where to beam the signal and Mallica had added her part in Swooshian.

Bram complimented the four of them for having developed a beacon. He likened it to a light house beacon to warn ships about dangerous waters but in their case, they had developed a beacon to guide his ship into a safe harbor. He also pointed out that by beaming light, Pat had confirmed that the magnetrons would be able to transmit video.

He asked whether it was five in the morning or five in the evening.

Pat pointed to everyone in the hanger and said that they had all rushed to the hangar when word got out that you had returned. It has been a stressful time, but everyone continued to focus on their work and in your absence a phenomenal amount of work has been done.

She replied that it was five in the afternoon and that it was time to go home.

I am looking forward to sitting next to you on our dual recliner and listening to the tales that I am sure you have to share.

Linda asked if she could announce a day off and a picnic at the community center. She said that her parents were ready and eager to hold such an event. They said they would expect that they would get an invite to a Sunday breakfast where they could hear what he had learned.

Bram said he had no clue as to what day it was, but he suggested that they make the picnic on Saturday, and he would welcome the Stetson family for breakfast on Sunday.

Linda let him know that it was Thursday, and that Saturday would be perfect.

Pat guided Bram toward the side hangar door.

He realized that he was walking a pleasant gauntlet of friends welcoming him back. Every one of his close supporters were giving him praise for having come back safe and alive.

Once he was in the van, the convoy moved out and made its slow way toward his house. Zoe said that he looked like he had lost weight.

Fold Wormhole

Bram replied that he had eaten as best he could, but Pat had just underestimated the amount of food he would need.

Eric commented that he was lucky that everyone added to the original order. He asked how the sixpack that he had put in the frig went down.

Bram chuckled and said that he had celebrated each time he got closer to the light and the last sip went with the last bite of food. He said that the beer was great.

Bob greeted them as they got out of the van and said that the Chateaubriand was just coming out of the oven, and everyone should go directly to the dinner table.

Bram thanked him and said that he was taking the elevator to his room and taking a quick shower, and he would be down in five.

It was a marvelously delicious dinner. It reminded him of the story of stone soup where all the people of the village contributed an ingredient so to a soldier who had volunteered to make a special stone soup. He put in the stone and the villagers kept giving him food items to add to it. In the end the soup had been fed to a hungry village that complemented the soldier for making such a delicious stone soup.

That triggered his memory about a Vietnamese story about a King who felt that he had not eaten well for a long time, and he put up part of his kingdom as a reward to the person who would feed him the best meal. All the famous chefs tried their hand and failed.

The King was out for a ride when a peasant said he was in the middle of preparing one of the best meals in the world. He invited the King to share it with him.

The peasant began by putting a water filled iron pot over the fire and added pieces of really tough meat. He suggested the two of them go for a walk while the meat cooked.

On returning from the walk, he added rice and stirred it in.

He sat and talked with the King about the tough life he had lived and the family that he had raised.

He kept checking the pot and as the day came to a close he said it was not quite ready. He offered the King his bed and took his place on the floor.

The next morning, he once again checked the pot and put in a head of chopped cabbage and cut carrots into chunks and added them.

He once again took the King for a walk. This time they walked along the canal, and the farmer threw in a baited line attached to the end of a bamboo pole and handed it to the King.

The King hooked and pulled in a rather nice sized fish. He commented that he had never been fishing before.

The farmer complimented the King on the prize fish he had caught and carried it back. He prepared it to put into the stew.

He then pointed out that it was rather late, and it would be better to wait until morning when everything would be cooked to perfection.

Fold Wormhole

By the third day the King commented that he was really getting hungry.

The farmer dropped the fish into the stew and shortly he had a thick bowl of rice laced with soft sliced cabbage with the cooked fish the King had caught. He put the bowl of gruel in front of the King and suggested that he put the salty, fish sauce mixed with red pepper over the gruel.

The King took one bite of the steamy hot gruel and declared it the best food he could remember eating.

The peasant was granted his piece of land and became a close friend of the King.

Pat knew that Bram was off somewhere in his head and reminded him what he had agreed to during dessert.

Chapter 5 Political Driving Force

The dessert discussion led to a political discussion when Zoe asked what he was going to do about the oversight committee that the Senate had approved.

Bram looked over to Pat and asked how the city building on Gaia was going.

Pat shared that it was eighty percent in place. The power source was generated by wave water and would support a city at least three times the size of the present one that was near completion. She went on to say that the lab would be the most advanced one that the Fold organization would have.

Zoe asked who would be on the list to move there.

Bram replied that his bodyguards could make that choice, but he asked that they remain as his local bodyguards until the moment that he permanently made the transfer to Gaia.

Pat then smiled and said that she and Amy had run a contest to see what the planet's name should be. They took everyone on a visual tour of the planet that had been selected. She said that the visual tour was very beautiful and awe inspiring.

The new world inspired a mirid of names and Mataia (Ma ta ee ah), meaning awesome, won the contest.

Bram shook his head and said that he wanted to see the video tour of Mataia so that he could get used to the name of the planet. He then asked what their star and solar system was called.

Pat replied that those names were still under consideration because they had spent the rest of the time looking for him and didn't have time to manage the next naming contest.

Bram thanked her for focusing on guiding him back and asked how she had figured out how to find him.

Pat smiled and said that intuition and luck had played the biggest part, but she credited Remi and Marcus for providing her the message and the coordinates to direct the beam too. She went on and explained that they had beamed twenty-four hours a day for more than a month during their search for him and that all of his bodyguards had participated in keeping the beam going.

Bram again thanked everyone and said it was good to be back.

He said that their work had provided him a way to try to see if he could explore negative Fold with bubbles that were equipped to look for and then follow the message beam back to a Fold point that would let them fold back to their launch location.

He figured that he would most likely lose a few bubbles before he figured out the exact way to enable the bubbles to return.

Fold Wormhole

Zoe made the snide comment that he could go out a few more times personally to make sure his method worked.

Bram smiled and said he would need to look again at the folks that qualified to migrate to the Mataia. He said he felt like giving her a hug for once again being willing to virtually tweak his nose.

The next day at work, Erica came to his office and asked if he was willing to discuss how to handle the oversight committee that had been approved and was in the process of having members selected and approved by both political parties.

Bram said he was eager to discuss the strategy they should follow and how slowly they should educate the committee. He made the point that they had made so many breakthroughs that they needed to manage how to share those breakthroughs and who should be the face that shared them.

He said he had no interest in dealing with that committee after their initial on-boarding.

Erica agreed and said that she had no desire to be the face either.

She suggested that Jeffrey would make the best face. He had the political connections and had developed a close relationship with the current administration. She went on to share that John Morgan had recently told her that he was planning to retire and that he had been asked to be part of the oversight committee but had declined.

Bram asked if a message to the President suggesting that he designate Jeffrey as the next NASA director would help.

Erica said that it would make a significant difference since she had learned that there were two other qualified people on the short list. Neither of the two were familiar with the Fold effort.

Bram asked Erica to stay so they could immediately put together the message to the President.

Bram penned the message and ask Erica for her input.

He incorporated her suggestion of making the point that Jeffery had intimate knowledge of the Fold project and would make the best candidate that would bring a wealth of knowledge that he could use to educate the oversight committee.

Once the message was sent, Bram suggested they get an early lunch so he could get together with Remi and Marcus and plan out the continued exploration of negative Fold.

Pat joined them on an early lunch. She asked if the two of them wanted to take a quick tour of the city on Mataia.

Bram asked what the city name was going to be.

Pat smiled and asked Erica what the name was. Erica smiled and said that she had won the naming contest with the entry, Einstein City.

Bram gave a small laugh and said that the name was an excellent choice. He asked how long the tour would last.

Pat replied that they should spend a couple of hours but that a full tour would take closer to a full day. She went on to say that a day on Mataia was twenty-five hours long.

Fold Wormhole

Bram suggested they take the short tour at the end of the day so he could get himself reoriented before the tour.

Remi smiled when Bram walked into the lab. He and Marcus had been discussing their success at having reached Bram and given him a beacon back.

Rem shouted out, "The quick brown fox who jumps through negative space is back."

The entire lab cheered and then clapped and shouted, "The Fox is back."

Bram smiled and thanked everyone and then sat down next to Marcus.

He more quietly thanked both Remi and Marcus for having spent the hours that they had in trying to get him back from negative space.

He then commented that in their current universe, time on the macro level always ran in one direction. It was always away from the time of the big bang. But on the micro level of electrons and quarks, time had no direction and could not be detected. He admitted that he had no clue as to why that was so, but it was so.

He then shared that in the negative space universe, time was present, but on a macro scale it had no orientation or direction. Its direction seemed to be random in nature. He was sure it was not random but followed a non-linear pattern.

He said that in trying to return, he had visited the Earth, but it was at the time when the single continent of Pangea existed. He then went out to Mars and discovered that at that time there was a sea that covered much of the planet, and it appeared as if there was plant life in the water.

He had traveled back in time!

That was something that was impossible in their universe where time always flowed forward.

Marcus asked how he had been able to position himself where he could receive the signal being sent out from their current universe.

Bram reminded them that Pat had put the bubble being used to send the transmission halfway into the negative Fold space and kept the other half in the positive Fold space.

He pointed out that what she had done was create a hole between the positive universe and the negative one. This let the signal being sent to originate from a single point in the negative universe.

He had been lucky to have folded to the distant galaxy home of the alien planet, Swoosh. He arrived there before their sun began to die. He then tried the coordinates of the dry worlds that had been found and then returned to Swoosh and this time it was near the time that the Swooshian's had sent out their call for help. It was close enough that a blinking light was at the far horizon of the on-board screen.

It was morse code blinking, "The quick brown fox jumped over the lazy dogs back," followed by, "I have your back."

It took me many tries to get close enough to that time in order to have the coordinate for the hangar to take effect.

I think you would put the entire return into the category of a miracle.

It is one that I know was supported by all but driven by the two of you and Pat.

Remi made the point that Pat was driving everyone to come up with any idea that might be of help. It was Mallica that suggested using Folded light to transmit the signal. He had suggested the fox message and Pat added "I have your back."

He pointed to Marcus and said that all Marcus had done was to give them thousands of coordinates to send the message to. In fact, the way he figured it Marcus had supplied several hundred thousand coordinates just to test the ability of the supercomputer system.

Bram asked which coordinate had worked.

Marcus replied that there was no way for them to know. He admitted to having set up a random coordinate generator to send out as many signals as the supercomputer could generate.

He smiled and suggested that Remi was just jealous that the random coordinate generator had worked.

Bram smiled and thanked the two again for having saved his butt.

He then asked if they would lead the effort in exploring the negative universe with bubbles. They would have to figure out how to send out bubbles and then retrieve them. After conquering that aspect, the negative Fold space could provide a look back in time.

He then threw out the possibility that they might be able to look to the future in the negative Fold universe. If they could, he doubted that they would be looking at the same world if they looked at Earth. He commented that if they could, then they could all get rich by playing the stock market.

Marcus smiled and said that Bram had a conniving part of his mind as well as the genius part. He said that he would enjoy exploring the negative Fold universe.

Remi said he would love to, but he had his hands full setting up his new lab, but he was really curious to see what the actual color of the dinosaurs' were.

Bram then brought up the oversight committee. He said that he was holding a meeting in two days to discuss how to bring that committee on board and what to share at what time. He said that he did not want them to learn about all their efforts at one time and there were several areas that he did not want to share until some distant future.

Remi smiled, looked at Marcus and added that Bram also had a shrewd section in his brain as well.

Fold Wormhole

Bram smiled and said he was discovering totally unused space in the voids of his mind that the two of them were pointing out.

He looked at the clock and realized that it was time for the tour to Mataia that he was looking forward to.

He asked Marcus and Remi if they wanted a quick tour of the new city on Mataia.

They both said that they were eager as well as ready.

Bram led the three out to where Pat was awaiting them. She said that the three of them made for a full load. She said that Amy was staying behind to monitor the Fold and be there when they Folded back.

The coordinate for the arrival location was inside of what was designated the Arrival and Departure terminal.

Bram commented that the terminal had not been an item on his original list.

Erica shared the fact that Pat and Amy had made substantial improvements and had requested many items that had not been on his original list. She commented that they had practiced his bad habit of wanting it yesterday and had hounded her for every additional item.

Pat gave a small laugh and said that she had only gone after the critical things. The power generation system was one of those requests. She praised Erica for having found and delivered the water powered system and the resources that helped them install it.

Pat led the group around the housing complex that featured homes with spacious yards that had plantings. Every street was paved and had sidewalks.

Bram asked how she had managed to get the infrastructure in place.

Pat admitted that currently there was no water, no activated sewage system, and no electricity. The streets, sidewalks and light poles had all been Folded into position.

She pointed at Marcus and thanked him for his ability to exactly position every item.

Marcus said that he had only used the coordinates that she and Amy had provided and then adjusted them for the fact that both the Earth and Mataia were in orbit and spinning.

Bram commented that he was impressed with Marcus's mathematical ability.

Marcus replied that the supercomputer and the programing abilities of Linh and Duong had allowed him to write an initial algorithm that could be used over and over.

Pat led the group to a large building that had a sign designating it as Fold Work Center. It was another structure that Bram commented he had not specified.

Erica said that it was a building that had been folded from a location on Earth where it had been standing. It was actually a structure that was a couple of years old and had been purchased for a song. It had been scheduled to be demolished so that a housing complex could be built on the site.

Fold Wormhole

She had arranged for a building mover to set the entire structure up for moving. The building movers said they were not equipped to move any building as large as she was asking to move. She told them she was not asking them to move it but to set it up for a move.

She then worked with Marcus about the Fold to move it.

She gave the basement and footing information to Pat.

Pat said she had worked with a contractor to pour the footings and the basement walls above ground just outside of the Fruit Barn. She was told that they had never done anything like she was asking for, but they would do it.

She said that getting the hole dug was the hardest part. She confessed that she and Amy had learned how to automate a backhoe to dig a basement. They had repeatedly used it to dig basements for all the homes. Then it came time to do the big basement for the Work Center.

Then we automated a bulldozer and a bucket loader. We now possess a fleet of automated heavy equipment whose control programs we continually improve.

Pat added that they had learned the hard way that the shovel, spade, and hoe were still tools that they could not automate. They also automated a ground tamper and an electric generator to supply power.

Bram shook his head. He commented that he was amazed that they had found the time to do it all while he was wandering lost in time and space.

Pat commented that there was nothing else for her to do and both she and Amy figured that they would need new skills beyond being certified astronauts that were no longer needed as bubble pilots.

They felt they had achieved the status of city builders, and certified heavy duty equipment operators.

Remi walked into the lab and stopped. He commented that he was ready to stay. He asked who had specified the lab layout and all the test equipment.

Pat laughed and said that he had. She reminded him of the time he had shared what should be in the Lab and how it should be laid out. She waved her hand around the room and said he got what he had asked for. Or she corrected, that he had what she had heard and recorded.

Remi again said he was ready to stay.

Erica commented that Bram had paid a pretty penny for all the latest lab equipment.

Bram replied that it was a pretty penny well spent. He said he was impressed with everything that he had been shown so far.

Pat led them up to the top floor of the building. The view of the ocean in one direction and the view of the mountains in the other and then the long beach line in the two other directions made them all stop and take a deep breath.

Pat commented that she had made the entire floor plan open and that every desk had an amazing view in three-sixty.

Bram said he wanted to join Remi in staying.

<h1 style="text-align:center">Fold Wormhole</h1>

Marcus spun around and said he had never been in an office that made him feel so invigorated and ready to stay at work.

Erica gave Pat a hug and said that she too was so impressed with what had been accomplished and she was ready for the next request.

Pat replied that in another month everything would be in place and the ability to stay would be real. And her next request would be the furnishings for all the homes and the offices.

Erica said that it would be no problem because Bram had a bottomless expense budget.

Bram nodded and said that they might as well live big and get the best of everything. He commented that he was sure both Amy and Pat would earn the title of genius interior decorators.

He walked over to Pat and gave her a hug. He commented that she had proved to be more versatile and effective than he could ever be.

He said that his Fold back was anticlimactic after seeing what she and Amy had done with their 'spare' time.

Bram walked over to Amy and thanked her for being the best desert pilot that he had ever known and that on Sunday he was having a special breakfast for all his personal pilots.

When they got back Linda reminded Bram that she had everything set up for a big lunch starting at high noon at the pool side club house.

She had gotten the two Marine bands and a guitar player to provide entertainment. She said it would be one of the best attended events that they had held. She knew that Jeffrey and his family would be in attendance and there might be others that were coming in.

Bram thanked her for the heads up.

After they got home, he said that he preferred a light snack and then he wanted to spend time in his office before getting to bed early.

He had missed sitting with Pat and was looking forward to sipping on a glass of sparkling water and having Pat laying against him and reading.

He commented that he enjoyed having a person of gigantic capability using him for a pillow.

Pat replied that she enjoyed leaning against a fearless though somewhat mindless genius who could solve the most difficult problems but could not recognize the danger and go mindlessly into an unknown environment.

Bram woke up early Saturday morning and after a quick shower he went down the two-person elevator to his office. He was deep into the mathematics of a rhombicosidodecahedron (RCDH) diagram when the office door opened, and his four bodyguards and Pat more or less burst into his office.

Fold Wormhole

They said that they had worried about where he was but had listened to Pat who had assured them they would find him in the office with either a bubbly glass of sparkling water or a cup of tea.

Eric reminded Bram that he was to have two of his FBI body guards with him at all times.

Bram apologized and pointed to the two persons lift and suggested they put a Bram alarm on it because he had come down from his bedroom and he had immediately gotten into his negative Fold investigation and not thought for a moment about bodyguards.

He chuckled and asked them where they had been when he had needed them during his wandering in the proverbial negative Fold desert looking for the promised land.

Zoe shook her head asked if he wanted brunch.

Bram asked the time. Pat said that it was the same as the time shown on his computer. She smiled and said that he could believe his computer when he stayed in the positive world.

He pushed a button, and the large screen came on showing a screen full of equations and a series of mathematical symbols with scribbling. There was no computer time anywhere. He then asked again what time it might be.

Pat pointed to the wall clock and said that it was not the mechanical clock that he had relied on for more than a month, but it was showing real Earth time.

Bram smiled and said he had not looked up since he had glued his eyes to the rhombicosidodecahedron and started to break it down into a series of equations.

Zoe asked him to speak to them in English and not negative Foldeese and what was his answer to having brunch.

Bram shook his head and said that what he preferred was to shut down his computer and get the rhombicosidodecahedron out of his mind and walk down to the club house and see if Ted and company had any snacks and maybe he would ask Eric for a recommendation on what beer was the best to drink with a brat.

Bob commented that all four of them would be on duty during the picnic. He said they did not expect any attacks but that had been the case before every attack. He and Thomas had met with the General who had his observation team active, and they would be monitoring the area around the Fold compound looking for anything out of the ordinary.

Thomas commented that Bram's Marine bodyguards and every off-duty Marine would be present as well at the picnic. Their armament was stored in the back of the club house in a van.

Bram commented that he was surprised at the level of protection.

Pat said that Lacy had put out a warning that her network of listeners had picked up some discussion about eliminating Bram before he created a situation that would crash the financial market.

Fold Wormhole

Bram smiled and said that they were too late, and he had already let the cows out of the barn. They should be happy to learn that the cows had tall grass to go through, so they were moving out slowly.

He stood up and said that he was now certain to need a beer or maybe two. He started for the door and Bob got out ahead of him and told him to follow him to the Club house.

When they stepped out of the house they were surprised to see Orlando standing next to Castor and Donna. Orlando was in a First Lieutenant Marine Officer's uniform.

Bram stopped and commented that he had never touched a Marine Lieutenants' Eagle Globe & Anchor Pin and slowly did so. He pointed at the Expert Rifle pin and commented that he had witnessed that expertise as it saved his life. He pointed at the Jump Parachute with wings and a machine gun across it and said that it would frighten anyone on the ground to watch Orlando coming down from the sky at them. He pointed to the Pistol expert pin and commented that he had witnessed Orlando shoot the fly off the top of his beer bottle and then take sip from the lips of that same beer bottle.

He smiled and then gave Orlando a hug and congratulated him on getting promoted.

Orlando gave a salute and said that he was promoted because of Bram's recommendation to the General that had suggested making him a Captain.

Bram smiled and said that he always did get confused by military ranks.

He then pointed to Castor and his new USMC Sergeant Major of the Marine Corps uniform and said that if he shot the next attacker before he the attacker could shoot one of them he would put in his recommendation to the General to the next rank.

Castor replied that he and Orlando had been together when they talked with the General who had made it clear that Bram had made his recommendation all the way up to the Chief's of Staff who had then called him to ask what Orlando, and he had done to received such a recommendation.

Zoe said that Bram valued being kept alive and protected and that he had a similar impact with his FBI bodyguards who each were promoted in place and had to turn down jobs at other locations so they could get him to keep sending in recommendations.

Orlando turned and said that it was time to get to the rec center. He said he would lead the way and make sure the bar got opened.

They were the first group to show up.

Bram walked over to Tom and after shaking hands asked if there might be a brat or two available.

Tom said that he had brats, sausages, sliced and barbequed brisket.

Bram asked for a brat and a sausage. He said that he was sure to have some brisket later.

Fold Wormhole

Tom said that Rita had also prepared ribs, steak, and sirloin for the main course. He said that she kept asking what Bram might want the most.

Bram walked over to where Rita and her sister Marial were setting up the food tables. He gave them both a hug and then complemented them on the food they were preparing and that it looked and smelled delicious.

He promised that he was going to take at least a bite of everything.

Cedric had just put a dish of sweet potatoes down and came over and gave Bram a handshake. He commented that Bram had just made his wife and her sister very happy with his promise to try a little of everything.

The members of the community started to arrive.

The Marine Band set up and played classical background music.

One of the younger members of the community asked the band if they could play songs that would support the Harlem shake.

The Marine Band switched to the music that supported the Harlem Shake.

Bram was surprised by Zuri who gave him a hug, took his arm, and said that she would teach him the Shake.

Bram laughed and followed her to the dance floor. He did not wait but went into his version of the Harlem Shake.

When the music changed to "Teach me to Dugie," he did his version and again surprised Zuri who was laughing and shouting that she had found a closet dancer.

Then the DJ announce that the next song should be done in a Conga line and Bram decided that he would sit and watch. He saw that Orlando was in front and that Elizabeth was holding on to him. He was surprised to see Jina holding on to Elizabeth.

Bram saw that Pat and Amy were in the line, so he got up and broke in and got between them.

The dancing stopped when Ted announced that the food was served, and it was time to picnic.

Each table had a number on it and the food line went in the order of the table number.

Bram had selected the table whose number put him in the middle. He had made sure his bodyguards got one of the first tables.

Lacey and Linda had asked to sit at his table. Linh and Duong were also at his table and the last two were Orlando and Mallica.

Orlando commented that he had been asked to write a ditty about a mad scientist that was willing to risk his life by venturing into the unknown. He asked if anyone had any ideas about the wording.

Pat said she had a few words, but she could not share them in public.

Chapter 6 Negative Fold Scouts

The Sunday breakfast was fully attended. Bram was doing the cooking. He used extra blueberries and chocolate chips in the pancake mix and got great feedback on how great they tasted with Maple syrup and butter. The sausage patties on the side were consumed at a high rate.

Bram felt good about being able to serve the core of the people that had rescued him from the negative Fold world. He knew that he was the living example of what great teamwork could do.

He had worked with Pat to set up a video to share once breakfast ended. The lead in was a tour of Mataia, and Einstein City.

The Entire Stetson family, the Juma family, Marcus and his kids and a few other folks were in the dining area. If he had offered he could have filled the community center, but he wanted to share some information that he did not want to be widely know at this time.

Pat took over and said that unless someone had a better name, the city she was going to show was going to go by the name Einstein City. In time she said it would be the capital of Mataia, the planet that had been selected to house the Fold operation and its community. She shared that the solar system was at least two light years away and it had six planets. Mataia was the fifth planet out and the only one that appeared to be habitable, but she said that they knew very little about that system.

Pat and Amy had used a camera drone and had done an excellent job of mixing longer range shots that zoomed in and then gave close ups of many nature sights and also showed the details in Einstein City.

The tour impressed everyone, and Pat and Amy got tons of positive feedback and many questions about the plantings that were around the yards. Amy made the point that no Earth plants had been Folded to Mataia and that all plantings came from that planet. She stressed that up to this point plant life was the only life that had been found.

Pat made the point that everything Folded to Mataia had been sterilized in an attempt to keep from contaminating it. She said that she and Amy had installed an ultraviolet light gate that everyone went through when they arrived on Mataia and that those arriving walked across a rug saturated in disinfectant to prevent contaminating Mataia.

Fold Wormhole

The presentation then transitioned to the Negative Fold realm. Bram shared how disoriented and how amazed he was that time seemed to be non-linear and that it did not flow in one direction as it did in the Universe that they lived in.

It instead seemed to randomly move based on the coordinates that a Fold was using. He commented that for him the mechanical clock keeping time in the bubble was the only thing that had let him know the actual time that had passed. It had allowed him to keep him from losing his cool. He admitted that the length of time that he had remained lost exceeded all of his expectations. He pointed at Pat, Linda, and Chef D'Carluca and said that the food they had all put into the bubble kept him from starving.

He then pointed to Marcus and said that all the coordinates that he had dutifully recorded provided a means of slowly getting closer to the time of his home universe. He had learned how to get back to his time, but he had also figured out that return by that route to his start time on Earth was beyond his lifetime.

He then pointed at Mallica and said that her use of transmitting light via the Messaging Fold Magnetron and Pat's ingenious use of well used phrases sent by old fashioned morse code provided the means to get back to the positive time universe. It became the beacon safety that he followed in via many more Folds than he had anticipated.

He looked around the dining area and said that they were all welcome when it came time to Fold to Mataia with him.

He said that such a move would only occur if it seemed they were losing control of the Fold program. He made the point that discovery of new capabilities had come so quickly and there was every possibility that new discoveries would continue, and he felt that oversight would most likely become very political and hinder progress.

He made the point that negative space, where time was random in its flow, might also lead to the ability to move forward in time and see the future. If such a thing existed it would be very troubling from a social-political point of view. It would be an ability that would make life as they knew it uncertain and more like a pool of quicksand.

He said that they and a handful of others would need to do a lot of exploring and development in order to understand all the breakthroughs on which they were working.

He pointed out that politics was now taking a first step into the Fold effort that so far had been a non-political effort. He made the point that there was no stopping it, but it was incumbent on them to manage it so that the power associated with the ability to Fold was somehow kept in balance and used for positive endeavors.

The next day, he Marcus and Remi met in Remi's new lab located by the Fruit Barn. They were setting up the lab to be where Marcus could launch and retrieve the scout bubbles that would be sent into the Negative Fold environment. The goal was to minimize the exposure of the effort but set it up for success.

Fold Wormhole

Bram suggested they first use tethered bubbles that they could physically retract. He said that by repeatedly sending them out they might be able to map what was happening and how to control the bubbles.

He said that having the control bubble halfway into the Negative space area as they had done to rescue him and having that bubble held in place with three bubbles in normal space would provide the halfway bubble the stability needed to pull the negative space exploratory bubble physical back.

Together they designed and outfitted the control bubble and got the exploratory bubbles equipped. By the end of the week, they had the effort organized and ready.

Bram said that as soon as they learned how to control the exploratory bubbles he would step back, and Marcus could then determine how to explore the negative Fold arena. He asked that when Marcus learned how to direct the exploratory bubbles they all get together and figure out how to set up a control system that allowed the exploratory bubbles to move about on their own.

Pat and Amy had spent the week in continuing the development of Einstein city and Erica had delivered all the office furniture and artwork that could be hung to provide some break in the open office area.

Erica had made the point that the water treatment work had been a challenge since they were having the local contractors do the work normally done down in a hole in the ground out on a flat surface near the Fruit Barn building. After it was complete and the appropriate hole dug in Mataia, they would Fold the object into the hole.

She credited Pat and Amy with getting the exact coordinates needed at the moment of transfer and with Marcus's ability to hit those coordinates within a few millimeters.

She commented that she was impressed at his ability to hit a moving target more than two light years away so accurately.

Marcus had admitted that the movement of the solar system that Mataia was in and the movement of the planet itself had made identifying the exact coordinates a challenge. He shared that he and Mallica had come up with the equations that determined the transfer coordinates that the supercomputer generated just before the Fold. He said that so far it seemed to deliver the objects within plus or minus a half a centimeter.

Bram commented that such a feat was simply mind blowing since on Earth a tolerance that tight was seldom achieved in general construction.

Amy said that she and Pat were always amazed when their prefab objects popped into existence exactly where they needed them. Even after having moved several hundred large objects into position and doing several thousand smaller Folds they were still in awe that they could construct an entire city.

Fold Wormhole

They joked that the most work they had done was to program and automate several pieces of construction equipment to do the heavy work but had failed to automate the basic shovel.

Amy let out a pretend groan and bent over with her hand on her back. She said that Pat was forgetting all the pick, and the spade work they had so far endured during the city building.

Bram smiled and commented that he had wondered about Pat's six pack abs and her muscle-bound shoulders. He thought she had bulked up just for him.

He then complimented them and said that the capability that they had developed would be priceless in setting up the construction business for the transition it would face in the near future. He suggested they document their learning and be prepared in the future to train the construction community in the basics.

Pat commented that the city now had running water and an operating water treatment plant.

They had set up each home with geothermal HVAC systems that also generated the electricity for each home. The geothermal system also provided the lighting throughout Einstein City. This approach provided the margin of power needed to support the Fold process.

Many systems on Mataia were in place and the water powered generator was capable of topping off the electrical consumption needs. She pointed out that some of those needs would be for the additional manufacturing that they might not have anticipated.

Bram asked if there were any overhead services and learned that everything was either underground or in the case of the local internet it was broadcast to each house from the light poles in the neighborhood.

He asked Pat if she had their home picked out and furnished.

Pat let him know that the house was near the beach. It was furnished and his home office would impress him. She said that when everything was ready they could take a vacation to their new home.

Bram said that he would love to do that and that she should plan on the activities that they would engage in for their Mataia vacation.

Pat said that she wanted the two of them to pick out the locations they would visit on each day of their vacation.

Bram said that he would enjoy going through the video of the tour she had documented and pick out those locations.

Pat shared that she had requests from several folks about doing something similar. She asked if Bram had any reservations about such vacations.

Fold Wormhole

Bram thought for a minute and suggested that she and Amy set up the protocol and that the folks that chose to take such vacations would adhere to a do not pick, disturb, or try to bring home artifacts of any kind.

Once back to the lab it became clear that the Folds into negative space was turning out to be a challenge. Even though tethered to the control bubble, the exploratory scout bubbles seemed to end up in random time periods and random locations.

Marcus had decided on a rapid mapping approach. He had determined the time it took for the bubbles to get to the end of their tether and had then pulled them back and reset them and then sent them out again.

The bubbles were going out at roughly five-minute intervals and Marcus was slowly plotting the pattern that they were making. He soon learned that the pattern was not random but followed the rhombicosidodecahedron surface that took on the size of where the Fold ended.

After making some forty Folds he realized that he was slowly forming multiple sixty-two-point rhombicosidodecahedrons that Bram had described.

Then he began to speculate on the coordinates of the next point based on the initial coordinates that the probe used. He hit a home run and knew that even on a tether, each Fold of the exploratory bubble took it to the next point on the surface of a rhombicosidodecahedron the size that was determine by the coordinates to where they had been sent.

This was amazing to him, and it also posed the next challenge and that was how the desired point on the rhombicosidodecahedron could be selected and a bubble sent to that specific point and then be brought back in a reasonable time frame by skipping the intermediate points.

Marcus asked Bram and Mallica to stop by to help him determine how to direct the bubbles.

Bram listened to Marcus and asked Mallica if she had any idea of how to proceed.

Mallica looked at Bram and said that she was ready to listen to whatever had just flashed through his mind.

Bram asked Marcus to pull up a diagram of a rhombicosidodecahedron. He then asked Marcus to put a small one on the left of the screen and a larger one on the right side of the screen.

He pointed to the small one and said that if they were to create a small launch rhombicosidodecahedron in their space and use each point as a launch point, he speculated that the exploratory bubble would go to the corresponding point on rhombicosidodecahedron in the negative space realm.

He went on to say that the size of the negative space rhombicosidodecahedron would depend on the amount of the time as measured in their space that the exploratory bubble traveled. Once it reached the comparable node it could be moved just as Marcus had learned to move the bubbles on his first round of sending them out.

Fold Wormhole

The return when triggered should bring the exploratory bubble back to the point corresponding to the next point of the rhombicosidodecahedron in normal space that corresponded to the point on the negative space rhombicosidodecahedron.

Marcus nodded and said that it would take him almost a month to verify Bram's thesis, but he felt sure that he would verify what Bram had suggested.

Mallica said that she was going to work on a program that an exploratory bubble could use to then move around negative space in a controlled fashion and then return after it made its designated round.

Bram asked Marcus to look up the amount of time that had been set on his very first Fold into the negative space.

He asked that Marcus begin with that time. Bram said that once they verified that they could control the exploratory bubble, he wanted to return to that ancient past of Earth and see what animals were roaming on Pangea. He speculated that the dinosaurs where predominant during that time.

Marcus said that if they learned to control the exploratory bubbles he would certainly want to become a bubble explorer.

Mallica nodded and said that a host of folks would pay dearly to be able to take such a vacation trip.

Bram gave a laugh and said that the two of them could set up a business of taking folks on negative Fold vacations to ancient destinations.

He speculated that they might be able to take folks to see a gladiator battle at the famous Colosseum arena in Rome.

Marcus said that it had just struct him that the negative Fold realm would provide archeologists and other scientists a way to go to the origin of their particular field and learn firsthand the facts they were trying to verify.

Bram nodded and said that such capability would certainly be sought by countless individuals. It would be knowledge that needed to be shared at the end of all the changes that the current society would undergo.

He suggested that they needed to learn if they could only see the events or if they could enter and participate in such events. That would be one of the capabilities they would need to determine. He said that it was a particular frightening thought if they were able to enter into that fabric of time.

He speculated that initially they would only be able to look but he was sure that a way to enter into that fabric of time could be discovered. He thought about his own temptation and decided that the ability to enter the fabric of time would be the last place he would investigate, and he would make certain that those after him would need to really hunt to get to that capability.

Bram brought up the fact that the negative fold universe was one that they should all keep secret for their lifetimes. The upheaval of all the other breakthroughs would be all that the world could handle in the next several lifetimes.

Fold Wormhole

Marcus, Mallica and Remi all agreed but Marcus said that he was personally going to see about the dinosaurs.

Bram said that every one of the primary participants of the Fold program would get a chance to learn firsthand about much of the ancient times.

Later when he shared the discussion with Pat she added that one of the biggest draws for her would be those moments mentioned in the bible.

That triggered the alarm bells in Bram's mind. He commented that the time of the human was especially worrisome. He pointed out that much of what everyone believed and that was a foundation of two thirds of the world's population might have many holes in the story they believed in.

Whatever they learned would need to be evaluated against creating a tear in the fabric of the current world social order. He pointed out that the changes that the Fold technology would create would be a dramatic strain on that social order and that adding a religious strain on the social system might be taking a jump into the abyss.

Pat said that she agreed and that she recognized that her eagerness was like a lemming rushing over the cliff in its eagerness to follow the ones in front of them.

Bram nodded and said that they were leading the millions that would follow, and they should relish what they were learning and then should carefully and slowly expose what they had learned to those that would follow them and those that would take their place.

Chapter 7: Family Feud

When Bram arrived to work on Friday morning, Remi was waiting and said he had to check with Bram to see if he had authorized anyone to take the exploratory bubble out.

Bram replied that of course he had not.

Remi said that the exploratory bubble was missing so either it was accidently Folded, or someone took it out.

Bram asked Linda to contact Marcus.

Moments later she said that she had no answer from Marcus and had not been able to leave a message because his phone was either off or out of range.

A feeling of concern went through Bram. He led the way back to Marcus's office. It was empty and it was clear that it had not been in use.

He then went back to the Lab where he and Remi had set up the negative Fold control computer. He refreshed the screen and pointed to the most recent coordinates. He said that he bet that those coordinates corresponded with Earth's location when there was only Pangea and that the early dinosaurs were roaming across its surface.

Bram activated the computer that he had used on his Fold into negative space and verified the coordinates of Earth close to that time. It was a close match.

Remi asked how they would get Marcus to return.

Bram replied that he was sure that Marcus would return on his own. He wondered aloud what might have caused him to take such a risk.

Remi shook his head and said only some extreme emotion would.

Bram led the way back to his office and asked Linda to contact Myla to see if she could find out what had upset Marcus.

Bram then led the way to the cafeteria. As he went past Linda's desk he mouthed where he was going.

He had been invited by Chef D'Carluca to taste a special cinnamon and cream Danish with which he was experimenting. Chef D'Carluca said that he would enter it into a cooking competition if he got a number of Fold personnel and Marines to say it was not only good but great.

He brought out two Danish that he had made that were still warm from the oven.

Fold Wormhole

Bram savored the sweet of the warm cream and found the surprise of warm blueberry flavor as he bit into the piece that he had cut and was slowly chewing. It was indeed great.

He was about to compliment Chef D'Carluca on the magical creation that he had come up with when he saw Linda entering the cafeteria.

It was clear that she was not delivering good news.

He put up his hand and stopped her from saying anything. He cut a liberal piece of his Danish and pointed for her to sit down and try the most wonderful treat she would ever taste.

He took another bite for himself and then finished with a sip of the tea that had accompanied the Danish.

Linda finished her Danish and commented that it indeed was the most delicious Danish she had ever eaten.

Chef D'Carluca was beaming and said that he would fix all three of them whatever they wanted for lunch.

Bram said he would settle for a small steak smothered in melted blue cheese. Remi and Linda put in their orders.

When Chef D'Carluca left for the kitchen, Bram looked at Linda and said that she could now share the sad news that she had walked in with.

"Your right, but it really is sad news," I learned that Myla had decided to end their marriage. She felt as if Marcus was wed to his work versus her.

Linda said she had asked about the kids and learned that Myla wanted to leave them with Marcus. She wanted to start anew. Linda then shared that she had asked if Myla had told Marcus about leaving the kids with him and found out that she had not because he had left as soon as she had made her declaration that she was leaving.

Bram looked at Remi and said that he had just figured out how to get Marcus back home. They were going to let him know about the kids.

He thanked Linda and asked her to arrange a meeting with Myla at her home and that he would go there as soon as they had sent a message out to Marcus.

He then led the way to the lab and asked that the negative Fold interface bubble be put in position.

He then typed in the phrase, "Get good dinosaur pictures. The kids are yours and waiting for you. Follow the light back." He put the transmission into a do loop that would repeat the message over and over and then he went back to his office.

Remi had agreed to stay in the lab and wait for Marcus's return.

At lunch he asked Pat if she had time to go with him to Marcus's house and talk with Myla.

When Pat asked what was up, Bram explained the situation. He said that he felt that they should intervene and see if they could make the transition easier on Marcus.

Fold Wormhole

Pat said that Amy could manage what the two of them were doing and that she would go with him.

Bram was silent as they took the short ride to Marcus's place.

Zoe and Eric had decided to be the ones to escort Bram.

Myla opened the door when Bram rang the bell. She stepped back and waved the four of them into the living room. She commented that it was like Bram to choose a face to face to find out what was happening.

She watched quietly as Zoe and Eric followed their normal routine of clearing the house.

Bram nodded and asked if the kids were in class. Once Myla verified that they were, he asked if her decision to leave was final.

Myla nodded and said that she had made the decision not so much about Marcus's work but more about the change that she had been experiencing as she attended her therapy sessions. She made the point that she felt as if she had arrived at many of her early life decisions based on her troubled past. She now wanted to experience the freedom she felt she had missed.

Bram commented that she was giving up lot to learn if that freedom, she was imagining, really existed.

Myla said she understood that and had discussed it in depth in therapy and had come to the decision she had made.

Her therapist had asked the same questions and given the same advice as he.

Bram then asked when she planned to leave.

Myla said that she was packed and ready to leave as soon as Marcus returned. She wanted to make sure the kids were safely in his care.

Bram asked whether he and Pat could have the kids for the afternoon until Marcus returned.

Myla asked from where Marcus would be returning.

Bram smiled and replied that was confidential, but Marcus would have real dinosaur pictures for the kids.

Myla shook her head and commented that Bram had just given her information that made her leaving easier and yes, the world in the Fold environment was one that held uncertainty and caused her anxiety.

She then said that he and Pat could have the kids for the afternoon or however long Marcus took to return.

She then thanked Bram for having helped in opening up the world for her. His support at just the right time had changed her and had given her new strength and would always be cherished.

Pat asked if she could arrange transportation.

Myla replied that Linda had called just before their arrival and had done so. Myla commented that Linda seemed to know exactly how this discussion would go.

When the honk of a horn interrupted the discussion, Myla stood and pointed to the three large suitcases that were in the corner of the living room.

She took one and asked if the two of them would push the other two to the door.

Fold Wormhole

Zoe led the way to the door and stepped outside and joined Castor and Linda.

Once Myla was on the way, Pat suggested they go by the recreation facility, where school was held, and meet the kids there and bring them to the house.

Bram agreed and said that they should have a special dinner prepared and that he hoped Marcus would make it back by that time.

He contacted Remi and asked him to bring Marcus to dinner and that he was invited as well.

Remi commented that he did not want to get involved in the discussion with Marcus.

Bram reassured him that the discussion with Marcus would happen after dinner in the privacy of his home office.

Once they had Marcus Jr. and Mylan home, they got Zoe to take care of them. He watched as Zoe suggested they get any homework due the following day done and then she would watch a movie with them.

Bram discussed the evening meal with Thomas who had the cooking duty. He was pleased that it was to be sweet spareribs, green beans, and mashed potatoes. It was the type of dinner that could be held for some time and still be served hot and fresh when the time was right.

He hoped that Marcus was able to follow the light which presented a short cut past all the nodes that time would take him through in the normal return sequence. It turned out light in the negative Fold realm actually followed a very precise rhombicosidodecahedron node pattern whose size was based on the distance of the first fold. Following that pattern might take centuries and perhaps even thousands of years if the first Fold distance was as far out as Marcus had gone.

The parallel rhombicosidodecahedron in normal space that they had set up allowed the short cut that he had postulated, and that Marcus was to verify. He hoped that his theory had been right and that a quick Marcus return would verify the theory. He smiled when he thought about how he had underestimated the movement in the negative Fold realm and how Marcus was personally going to verify the concept of using a parallel rhombicosidodecahedrons in normal space to understand negative space.

Dinner had been ready for forty-five minutes when Remi called to say that Marcus had returned and had been apologizing for his weakness.

Bram suggested that Remi remind Marcus about apologizing about decisions that he had made and that the two of them get a ride to his house since dinner was about to get served.

Fold Wormhole

Marcus's arrival pulled Marcus Jr. and Mylan away from a game they were playing with Zoe and Eric. He gave them a hug and then gave them each the dinosaur pictures that he had taken. The two kids took in the pictures and ask how he had gotten them and was the color of the dinosaurs the actual color?

Marcus spent a few moments sitting on the floor and talking to the two.

Bram declared that dinner was about to be served and everyone should fill their plates and then take their seats at the dinner table.

Pat guided the dinner conversation. She had the kids share how their day at school had gone and how they were doing in school.

When Mylan asked where her mother was, Pat said that Mylan would learn that from her father once they all got to their home.

Mylan nodded and a small tear ran down her face. It was clear she knew what was going on and that her mother had left.

Pat walked around the table and gave her a hug and whispered that she could come over at any time she felt like. She then gave Marcus Jr. a hug and made the same offer.

Bram complemented Thomas on the great desert.

Bob spoke up and said that desert had been his. It was a French version of Apple Strudel, but the Ice Cream was pure American.

Marcus Jr. said that it was the best desert that he had ever eaten.

Bram agreed. After a moment he asked Marcus to join him in his office. He led the way down the stairs to the basement where his office had been moved. He asked Zoe and Eric to wait outside of the office.

Zoe agreed but said that they would first check out the office. Bram led the way in.

Marcus stood quietly. He had the urge to apologize for his actions but knew that Bram would just stop him. He knew that he had broken a key trust and wished he had not done so.

Bram began by saying he was sorry for the emotional pain that Marcus was experiencing. He went on to say that Myla had expressed the fact that she still loved him but that she needed to go out in the world to experience the freedom that she thought she had missed.

Marcus said that phrase, "the freedom she had missed," kept reverberating in his mind. He thought of their marriage as a relationship that was bound in love and warmth and held all the freedom that anyone would wish for.

Bram commented that Myla had said she was waiting to make sure he understood that she was entrusting the children to him because he was a great dad and that he would teach them the fundamentals of having a good life.

Fold Wormhole

Bram then made the point that another unauthorized Fold journey would be his last. He reminded Marcus that it was strike two and there would be nothing in the Fold program after strike three.

He then suggested that they go back upstairs, and that Marcus take the kids home and explain what was happening. He suggested that Marcus send Myla a note letting her know that he would take care of the kids. Then he should take the kids on another weekend Fold vacation to where they could spend the time playing. He suggested a theme park and a beach.

Once upstairs, Marcus said thanks for the evening meal and then led the kids out the front door.

Bram and Pat watched as the three walked hand in hand toward their home.

Bram whispered to her that he wanted her to know that she provided him with the confidence to try anything. She was the bedrock on which he stood and the advice she had given him on how to handle the situation with Marcus had been dead on.

100

Chapter 8: A Fold Vacation

Pat turned to Bram and said that she was ready for the Fold vacation about which they had talked.

She shared the fact that Melisa had been traveling and locating Fold secure coordinates to be used to facilitate vacations. She had safe coordinates in most of Europe, the major parks in the US, Hawaii, and Alaska.

Melisa had asked if she should charge for the vacations and Pat said that she and Amy had suggested that there should be a charge that would pay for the cost of purchasing or renting vacation homes that had so far been contracted but the charge should be significantly less than that which tour groups charged for similar accommodations.

Bram suggested a meeting among the four of them and Erica to finalize how vacations were to be treated and get that approved. He said that Erica would manage getting the approval and once that was in hand the two of them would take a vacation through the northern arc of Europe and visit, Sweden, Norway, and Finland and then get warmed up with a stop in Rome.

Pat asked how long of a vacation he had in mind.

Bram replied that he figured a minimum of three weeks. He smiled as he said that a bubble-based approach meant that they would lose no time at airports so the time away would all be spent on enjoying the vacation.

The next day, the meeting was more of an articulation of the travel that Melisa and her husband had taken, as she went to each location and arranged for the housing, than a discussion of how to charge for the vacations. She explained that she had worked with local realtors to find a place at each location that she felt would work.

After either purchasing or signing a long-term lease, she worked with Marcus to determine the coordinates for the spot in one of the rooms that was designated the arrival-departure room. Marcus and she then tested each spot to ensure they had exact coordinates. She and Marcus had agreed to three tests to make certain that each location worked.

She smiled and said the bubble was empty for the first two tests but on the third test, someone from the team would transport in. She said that if they asked their closest co-workers they would learn that each had taken a one- or two-day mini vacation at the locations that were cleared to be used.

Once she had verified a location, she and her husband would take a weekend Fold there as they transitioned to the next location.

Fold Wormhole

Bram looked around the room and asked who had already tried the bubble vacation.

Erica smiled and raised her hand and said that she had been to the Rome bubble location and had gone to the Fontana di Trevi threw in her penny to make a wish. She pointed to Pat and said that she had made her wish come true. She added that she had also toured the Roman Colosseum.

Bram shook his head and commented that the most work driven person on site had escaped to Rome and played while the rest of the team worked their heads off.

Erica responded that she was number six in the string of folks sneaking off to get away from the hard driving mad scientist in the room.

The exchange ended when Linda entered the room and let Bram know that it was time for his meeting with Remi.

Bram asked her where her bubble escape had been.

Linda smiled and commented that the cat must have gotten out and yes, she and Lacy had gone to Stockholm over a weekend.

Bram smiled and said that he was pleased that everyone had become willing to evaluate the accuracy of the coordinates and that no one had ended up inside of a wall or buried in the floor.

Erica replied that they all had confidence that Marcus would have the right coordinates.

Bram went out to the van and his small army left the compound on the way to Remi's new lab. They had been working on an innovative approach to the transport bubbles that would make them less expensive to fabricate.

Remi had discovered that a ten-foot tube made of the same material as the current bubbles would be half the price and could be of any desired length. He had worked with the fabricator and modified the tube into a U tube. Remi was pleased with the fact that he would have a flat surfaced floor to work with. He had designed a variety of tube lengths that featured two, four, six and twelve seat versions. The seats were paired, and each seat had its own control screen. Each pair of seats were independent from the others, but all could control the tube.

Bram complimented Remi for the design that he was implementing. He suggested that a refreshment center be located in the back and that each seat had access to a place to put snacks and a drink.

He asked how many tubes of each size Remi had on order and learned that Remi was waiting for the two of them to decide.

Bram said he thought three tubes of each length would be a good start. Later, if the program grew, more could be ordered.

He suggested having one tube that could hold several Swoshians.

Fold Wormhole

Remi said that three of each size was what he had thought about as well and he had checked with Erica about such an order, and they had agreed to that number unless things changed during the meeting between them.

He said he would add the order for the largest one, but it would be for only one unit.

Bram agreed that was a good start. He said that he should contact Mallica to see if only one bubble for the Swooshian move was enough. He then asked if the bubble scout program was affected and learned that it was not and that scout bubbles were much smaller, and the cost of production was relatively low.

Remi commented that what was affected was the large bubbles that were being planned for the Alien transport. He commented that large enclosures made of two long J like extrusions mounted to a matching flat surface made making the very large vessels for the aliens much easier to make, assemble and to mount the interior equipment. The structure was much easier to work with than the bubble design.

When Bram asked about the assembly, he learned that it would be done in the same location as the first Swoshian bubble.

Remi then brought up the limitation that had surfaced was of getting the material to make the J and flat piece.

Bram suggested that the flat part could be of a different material and that the material from Mataia or one of the other discovered planets be directly Folded into a storage hangar at the producer's site.

Remi said that he would use each of the new tubes and make their first few trial runs, runs to transport the materials needed for construction of the next set of tubes. It would allow him to stress the vessels and not risk losing equipment or people.

Bram finally brought up the fact that he and Pat were going to take a rather long vacation and that he hoped that on his return the first new exploratory vessels were ready for trial.

Remi asked if they had decided on where they would go.

Bram replied that it would begin in Copenhagen then make a big circle through Norway, Finland, and Sweden and end back in Malmo, Sweden just across from Copenhagen. Then they would Fold to Rome and end the vacation there.

Remi wondered why they were going to Rome.

Bram smiled and replied that he was just trying to warm back up before returning to Dalles. He then added that Pat wanted to throw a coin into the Trevi fountain to wish for more vacations.

Remi nodded and said that he was with Pat on that.

Two days later he and Pat left for Copenhagen. Their Fold out was accompanied by their FBI bodyguards. Their bubble Folded into a large empty room of an apartment that turned out to be above a Sushi Bar.

Zoe and the rest of the bodyguards did a quick check of all the rooms. They then all walked slowly through the large corner apartment and admired both the design and the unique layout.

Fold Wormhole

Zoe commented that the kitchen seemed designed for a chef. The pots were all hanging and arranged by size and function. The knives were on a magnetic strip below the hanging pans. A glass cabinet displayed a myriad of spices.

Eric opened the stainless-steel refrigerator and pointed to a note that said they should enjoy the variety of Danish cheeses and sausages, and it gave information about each cheese.

The cheeses:

Danbo – Often called "Denmark's national cheese" made of slightly sour cow's milk. (PGI status)

Esrom – "Trappist Style cheese. It has "Protected Geographical Indication (PGI)" meaning it can only be made in Denmark.

Tilsit Havarti – also known as Danish Tilsit has an intense flavor and aroma

Bla Kornblomst – "blue cornflower" it is luscious, rich, and velvety organic cow's milk cheese that melts in your mouth

Mycella – This blue-green veined cheese with a sweet and savory flavor smoky over tone is made on the tiny Danish island Bornholm in the Baltic Sea between Zealand and the southern coast of Sweden

Vesterhavsost – "North Sea Cheese," Produced from the milk of west Jutlandic cows and ventilated by sea air for at least thirty weeks.

Danish Sausages:

Garnatálg – This sausage comes from the Faroe Islands. Garnatálg is a specialty prepared with cured sheep intestines and sheep tallow. The combination is shaped into large, oval pieces which are then air-dried.

Rød pølse – Sausage made with pork meat lightly smoked over beech wood. Created in the 1920s by resourceful vendors who would color stale sausages with red dye and sell them at a slightly lower price.

Medisterpølse - Classic Danish pork sausages prepared with pork, lard, onions, and a variety of spices such as cloves, allspice, and pepper.

He commented that they would need to go out and buy a selection of Danish beers and wines so they could enjoy the cheese and sausage.

Bram commented that Carlsberg was the icon Danish beer.

Pat commented that grape wine was a very recent thing for Denmark and that it had just recently become legal to produce there. Before the law changed only the European countries designated as grape wine producers could legally make commercial grape wine. They, however, had a long history of making apple and cherry wine as well as wine with other fruits. She suggested getting a bottle of each of them as well as a grape wine.

Bram suggested they go out shopping and get the appropriate amount of beverages and any other food they wanted to stock up with. He then said that on their return from shopping they should try the Sushi Bar before they came back up to their apartment.

Once back and well into the meal they were all eating at the Sushi restaurant, a meal that they were calling dinner, they discussed what they would do for breakfast.

They asked the waitress to recommend a place where they could enjoy a traditional Danish breakfast. She recommend a restaurant where they would be able to partake of the traditional Øllebrød breakfast. She explained that it was a porridge or thick soup made of sourdough rye bread and beer and that had a slightly sour-sweet, caramelly taste. She commented that the restaurant she was recommending had some of the best breakfast coffee as well.

She said that after breakfast a walk to see the Little Mermaid would help to digest the wonderful and very filling breakfast.

Fold Wormhole

Bram looked around the table and asked if everyone was up for a Danish breakfast. He said that afterwards he was planning a walk to see the Little Mermaid sitting near the entrance to the harbor.

Breakfast got a resounding yes vote and Bob said that he was really looking forward to the walk afterwards.

Bram had not mentioned that he had arranged for a van that would pick them up at the end of their morning walk to take them on a private tour to Copenhagen's most famous sites. He planned to have the driver meet them near the Little Mermaid statue.

Before Bram had left on vacation, General Tilson had approached him and suggested that he arrange for a Marine driver. He said he could have one at each desired location.

Bram had asked why the General was arranging for a driver and learned that the General was worried about his safety and that the van would be armored and the Marine a veteran of combat.

Bram had agreed and thanked him for thinking about it.

The General nodded and said he was just trying to protect the best assignment he had ever been given. He had let Bram know that he had made special arrangements for his drive from Oslo to Nordkjosbotn and that it would be the same driver as the one he would have in Copenhagen.

The Øllebrød breakfast turned out to be a big hit. Everyone kept umming and oohing and said that it was definitely a breakfast eating highlight though it was only a shadow of Pat's pancakes smothered in maple syrup.

Bram agreed and said that Melisa had arranged for a traditional lunch meal at a restaurant that he hoped would be as good.

Thomas asked what the lunch meal was called.

Bram said that he had Melisa write it down because it was a rather extensive menu that would certainly call for a really long walk.

He placed the handwritten menu on the table.

Zoe picked it up and read it.

Starter: a variety of Smørrebrød, which was buttered rye bread topped with any combination of meats, cheeses, and garnishes.

Main: Stegt flæsk med persillesovs, the "national dish of Denmark." It is a combination of crispy pork, potatoes, and parsley sauce.

Sides: Frikadeller, savory pork meatballs served with brown sauce, potatoes, and cabbage. Karbonader, breaded pork patties.

Desert: Rødgrød med fløde, a red berry pudding with whipped cream.

To drink: Your choice of beverage.

Fold Wormhole

Zoe ended by licking her lips and said that she was already hungry, and she had just eaten one of the biggest breakfasts of her life.

Bram agreed with Bob when he said he could hardly wait for lunch.

The walk from the restaurant took them through Langelinie park, a long narrow park along the harbor. The well-kept lawn seemed to call "sit your tush down for a moment and enjoy the feeling of my soft, thick coat."

The dark bluish green tree leaves provided shade as the sun rose slowly over the Swedish mountains rising above the building behind them. A warm breeze cooled by the cold water seemed to oscillate between being enjoyable and then chilling.

Bram pointed out that they would be Folding from their current apartment to one in Oslo that was about three hundred miles in the direction toward the eleven o'clock position from the Little Mermaid.

Pat held Bram's hand as they walked along the narrow part of the Park. She pointed ahead at the small statue of the Little Mermaid and commented that the bronze statue was just the right size and matched the vision she had of it.

Bram suggested that they continue the walk and go to the center of the park.

A very smartly dressed young man approached them and was stopped by Zoe and Eric.

He nodded and introduced himself as Marine Sergeant Matt Simple and said that a friend of theirs, Orlando had arranged for him to be the driver that would take them around Copenhagen and then he later would take them from Oslo up along the coast of Norway.

He pointed to where a black van was parked in the small circle a few hundred feet from where they were standing. He then said that Major General Lester Tilson had let Bram know that a driver would meet him at the statue of the Little Mermaid and that the General personally vouched for him.

Bram smiled and said he was looking forward to getting to know Matt better and to learn what he might have on Orlando.

Matt smiled and said that he had served with Orlando in combat and had some great stories about one of the bravest persons he knew.

Bram introduced Pat, Zoe, Eric, Bob, and Thomas.

Matt said that he had gotten reports on all of them and was impressed with all of them. He said that he had called Orlando and gotten his personal impression of all of them but the only thing he remembered at the moment was that he should not give Bram a weapon if he planned to shoot at anyone because Bram would wipe them out before he would have time to draw his own weapon.

Bram chuckled and replied that Orlando was known to often exaggerate a situation.

Fold Wormhole

Matt nodded and said that he had learned about the first shoot out at the cave by the Rushing River and how Bram had rushed to the front. He knew Orlando like a brother, and he knew that Orlando loved to tell stories, but Orlando did not ever exaggerated about a battle.

Bram pointed at the Van and said that it was time for them to begin the driving tour of Copenhagen.

Matt said that the FBI had cleared the tour guide. He was known as one of the best guides in the region and he was sure they would all enjoy his narration as they toured the route that he had been given.

Bram liked the fact that the van had six buck seats in the back and had windows all around. He and Pat had the two middle ones. Bob and Thomas took the two front seats and Eric and Zoe the two back seats.

The view of the outside was clear, and the tour slowly headed towards their lunch destination.

Ron Mueller

Chapter 9: Scandinavian Food

*L*unch was the highlight that they all had expected. There was no doubt that it was going to be hard to beat the flavor and the general goodness that they all enjoyed. They all agreed that it beat out sightseeing and that they could sit all afternoon and pig out.

Their tour guide commented that they had just enjoyed the best of the best of Danish food. He said that he had a recommendation for dinner that would compete with lunch but in a different manner. He suggested they try a wild game and seafood mixed dinner. He said the restaurant was owned by a friend of his and was named "The Mermaid" so it should fit in with the tour well. They had started at the "Little Mermaid" and would end it at a place named after a sister.

He said they should lead with two pork spareribs tide together with soften dried plums and pieces of apple wedged between them and then roasted.

He then recommended Svinemörbrad which he described as open-faced sandwiches. He suggested slices of cold roast veal, whole fillet of sole, smoked salmon that would be served on well buttered rye bread and would be garnished with cucumber, scrambled egg, or some other variety of greens.

He went on to say that desert should be Æblekage which was an old-fashioned Apple Cake, or they could try Brombærsnitter, or Danish Blackberry Cakes.

Bram looked around and asked if they were all in agreement to try out the dinner that had just been described.

It was a unanimous yes vote.

The tour guide asked them to give him a moment to call his friend to make the arrangements and then they would take a short walk around the neighborhood so he could point out the unique architecture of the buildings and the time the structures were first built. He added that it would also give them a chance to walk off a few calories.

On the tour the guide asked about the security provided by the FBI and did they expect something to happen.

Bram smiled and said that the last time they had come to Copenhagen, a rude Dane had insulted Pat and this time she had insisted on protection.

The guide frowned and started to say, "But I understood this was your first time… and then he laughed and said, Oh I get it. I am not supposed to ask."

Bram nodded and the guide said he hoped that in the near future he would find out who his mystery tour members had been and why they needed protection.

They returned to the van and the driving tour continued.

They visited the Zoo, The National Aquarium, The National Gallery, The Amalienborg Palace, The Round Tower, The Rosenborg Castle, Christiansborg Palace, Kronborg Castle, a UNESCO World Heritage site, and finally ended at the Botanical Garden. It had been somewhat of a whirlwind and all of them were ready to sit down and relax.

They then drove a short distance to Nylavn street that bordered a boat channel and had a variety of boats tied along its sides. The guide friend's restaurant was next to a popular outdoor steak restaurant. Three tables had been set up outside of his smaller restaurant to seat them.

Their arrival had been timed so that the first course that consisted of the open-faced sandwiches were first. Both beer and wine were also immediately served. It was clear that they were getting special treatment.

The view of the canal was captivating. Tied off near the restaurant were very elegant boats with people sitting out on deck and enjoying a casual snack or dinner.

Every boat had a combination of sail and motor power to propel them and were very well kept and had small gardens of flowers planted at various locations on the boats.

The buildings on their side of the canal ranged in color from the grey of their restaurant to reds, blue, yellow or had their original unpainted brown bricks. The buildings across from them were similar in color and variety.

A constant stream of people strolled along the street.

The conversation at the table centered on the sites they had seen during the day and the guide continued to provide information and adding information during the discussions.

Matt asked about the timing of their travel and when they were planning to leave Copenhagen.

Bram asked Pat if she had enough of touring around Copenhagen.

Pat said that she was ready to go on to Oslo and do something similar there.

Bram took out his phone and opened the folder that had the information about Oslo. He said that they had a top floor of a building on Bankplassen way.

He shared this with Matt who had informed them that he was their driver in Oslo and then all the way up through Norway.

Their guide, whose name was Sten Møller let them know that he would also be their guide in Oslo. He said he had lived there for years and began doing guided tours there. He smiled and said that he would enjoy helping them pick out great restaurants to try the local Norwegian food and added that he had connections in Oslo.

Pat asked where they should plan to have breakfast in Oslo.

Fold Wormhole

Sten volunteered that he knew a baker that made morning breakfast rolls and pastries for local restaurants and would most likely be glad to host them for a traditional Norwegian breakfast at his place. He pointed out that many of the very fine restaurants that were close to where they were staying did not open for an early breakfast.

He suggested they save the Café nearest to their place for an evening dinner and he would select a place for lunch that would fit with their tour.

Bram said that he liked the idea of relaxing and letting Sten make sure they got the best Norwegian meals.

Zoe asked if Matt would have a similar vehicle to tour them in Norway.

Matt replied that he was having his van shipped that evening to Oslo via a NATO transport vessel and it would be there for them to use the following day. He was going to ride with it to make sure.

He admitted that he had never had an experience quite like the one he was having and really wondered about who he was providing with a ride.

Bram smiled and replied that he was guarding a deviant from another galaxy who had invaded the Earth.

Matt laughed and said that he was ready to believe that it was something like that.

Pat chimed in and said that it was all about the ying and the yang of society. The two sides were always in a constant battle for control and at the end neither side really understood what the struggle was all about. However, it seemed that it was the little fish that always ended up on the hook and that the big fish never got on the line.

Bram shook his head and interjected and said that it was time to get to their apartment so that they would have time to finish their beer and wine and then catch their flight to Oslo. He recognized Pat's concern that had been triggered by Matt's comments.

That evening, Zoe commented that it was really hard to keep quiet about the Fold capability around Matt and Sten.

Bram agreed and said that he was finding it hard as well but that they had to maintain tight security. He pointed out that he was going to have to insist that the folks going on these Fold vacations begin to use the word special flight as the description for how they traveled about.

Eric threw in that he was happy to be able to sit and enjoy his beer and snacks, be able to get a good night of sleep and then in the morning Fold to the coordinates of their Oslo location. He said that he hoped to continue to be impressed with Melisa's selection of places.

Bram agreed and said that he had instructed Melisa to determine what should be charged for each location but that it should be at least forty percent less than that of the top end hotels.

Fold Wormhole

He commented that his bodyguards got a free ride and would actually earn income since they were on duty. He went on to say that after three beers or three glasses of wine they would have to declare themselves off duty and then the charges would quickly add up.

Zoe put on a sad face and asked if this was how he was going to get his revenge on her for her tweaking his nose.

Bram shook his head and said she was not even close, but she should make sure not to sleep too soundly when they returned to the Fold compound because she might wake up in negative space in a bubble with no food or water.

Pat sipped on her wine and said that the threats were getting a bit nasty and that she preferred they stick with deciding what they wanted to get out of their road trip through Norway.

Bram opened his notebook and showed the team the itinerary that Melisa had developed for them.

She had the ride beginning in Oslo, with a lunch in Donbas. The drive continued to Trondheim where they would stay for the night, and she had a set menu dinner reservation at the Trol restaurant that consisted of: Clam on the half shell, Trondheimssodd, Trondheim Soup, or Sodd, diced mutton meat balls, and a side of Norwegian flatbread. She suggested Stjørdalsøl beer and/or Karsk, coffee and moonshine.

She said they should set up breakfast when they registered at the Hotel Prinson.

She then suggested that they take plenty of snacks with them the next day and then go all the way to Grong where they could stop at the Garden Restaurant and do pizza or a wrap with ingredients of their choice.

They would then head to Fauske where they would have dinner and stay for the night.

Dinner would be at the Orlando Bar and Grill. She thought that would be appropriate because of their close friendship with their Marine friend Orlando. She recommended they keep the theme going and order the Orlando's House Steak, but it was their vacation, and they could choose to do as they pleased.

Their reservations for that night were at the Scandic Fauske Hotel. She suggested that breakfast be taken there and then they could drive on toward Bjerkaker where they could catch a late lunch and perhaps chose to spend the night.

But she had purchased a property up by Bardufoss out on highway Eighty-Six that had a large barn that could serve as a Fold site. She recommended trying to make it and then relaxing by taking a hike out into the forest.

Thomas said he was impressed with the suggested itinerary and that they Fold to their location in Oslo the following morning.

He added that a day or two in Oslo similar to their stay in Copenhagen would be enough and then they could relax, sit back, and enjoy the ride through the Norwegian countryside.

Bob added that he hoped that the food continued to be as good as they had enjoyed so far, and he suggested they add hikes at each of the stops they made so they would not balloon to double their size.

Pat agreed and asked that they all take some time and look at the cities and towns where they would stop and also the many parks and scenic areas they would pass and chose some key points of where to stop and hike.

She called up Google maps and began to follow highway six on which they would travel most of the time.

The discussion and the focus for the evening kept them all enthralled with what they were seeing. Zoe commented that she was really looking forward to the next leg of the vacation trip.

When they retired for the evening, Bram asked Pat how she was feeling about the vacation so far.

Pat replied that she was feeling very good, but she had the feeling that he had studied the trip much more thoroughly than she had anticipated and she was wondering what he might be holding back.

Bram shook his head. He said that he was holding back some information because he did not want to ruin the mood of wonder that he kept seeing from everyone as they discussed their experiences.

He admitted that General Tilson had some concern that the Marine spy knew about the vacation and that information might allow the big military fish he was trying to catch to take some sort of action. He was concerned that the long drive through Norway would provide some sort of opportunity for an attack.

The General had no specific intelligence, but he had taken every pre-emptive action he could take and was prepared to act immediately.

Bram added that as they drove along the highway, a US aircraft carrier would be sailing twelve miles off the coast with its fighter planes ready for takeoff. The General had been advised by his Admiral friend that the planes would always be less than five minutes away.

He then added that their driver Matt had been selected and assigned by the General. He was as much a war hero as Orlando and Castor.

Pat gave Bram a hug and said that he should tell the rest of the team so they could be as prepared as possible. She added that they were all professionals and did not need to be looked out for and it was their role to be on the lookout. She reminded Bram of having watched Zoe and Eric leap over the fence by the community pool in their skimpy swimsuits as they fired their weapons at the attackers. She pointed out that Bob and Thomas were immediately at his side providing additional support.

Bram nodded and agreed with Pat and said he would get them up to speed at breakfast the next day.

Fold Wormhole

Not long after, they Folded to Oslo.

Zoe led the inspection of the apartment and then called out the "all Clear." Then she led the way around the apartment. They commented that the apartment was as luxurious and well-appointed as the one in Copenhagen.

Eric added that he was impressed with Malisa's eye to location and to her taste in the decor of the apartments.

They went out to do a brunch and were met by Matt as they exited the building.

Bram welcomed him and invited him to have brunch with them. Matt replied that it would be great to get something to eat.

Matt commented that their plane must have special clearance for them to beat him. He had sailed all night long and had arrived with his van just moments ago.

They went out to the recommended bakery and were greeted by the owner who let them know that Sten had called to let him know of their likely visit for breakfast.

He took them to a table that he said he had moved into the front for them. It had a large variety of muffins and sweet rolls and plates of cheeses and sliced meat.

He had everyone sit down and then brought two pots of coffee and a pitcher of cream to the table. He then made sure everyone had what they wanted and then left them to what he called his slice of heaven.

After everyone was well into eating and enjoying the cheeses and sausage, Bram asked Matt what he knew about the drive-up highway six.

Matt replied that he had no information other than that it was his job to drive and make sure everyone remained safe.

Bram shared the situation of what they might face in the drive through Norway.

Zoe took a sip of her coffee and said that the vacation had just taken on some spice, and they would be looking at the forest and mountains with a much sharper eye. She asked why Bram was sharing the information so close to the actual drive.

Bram admitted that Pat had convinced him that they all deserved to be as prepared as possible. He had hesitated because there was no actual evidence of any preplanned attack.

Eric gave a small laugh and commented that so far, they had never received any intelligence giving them a heads up before a specific attack.

Bram acknowledged that fact. He credited General Tilson with arranging both US Naval and Marine support.

Thomas suggested they all enjoy the sites they had discussed the night before but be prepared for the unplanned and for anything out of the ordinary.

Matt nodded and said that what he had just learned, explained to him the armament in the back of the van that he had been issued. He said he had been issued and qualified on a new smart laser guided grenade that had wings and a range of more than a half a mile. And he had been issued a weapon very similar to an AK 15, but the ammunition was smart ammunition that would bend toward a hot target.

Bram said that he was not surprised about the weaponry. He had been told by General Tilson that they were taking no chances and wanted to make sure that if there was an attack that he and the Admiral had the upper hand.

Matt looked around the table and said that he had no idea why Bram needed to be guarded, but he would do all he could to make sure they were kept out of harm's way.

Zoe pointed to Pat and said that they were just trying to keep Bram and Pat from getting into any major personal disagreements.

Matt smiled and replied that Orlando told him that Pat was known to be fearless and that she always had Bram's back. He would wait and see how Zoe handled the disagreements.

Pat said it was time to get in the mood for their day tour of Oslo and asked if their guide was somewhere where they could pick him up.

Matt said that he had Sten's address and phone number and would give him a heads up.

Once they picked up Sten, they all spent the rest of the day touring Oslo, and they had lunch and dinner at the places that had been recommended.

The day had been a long one but a very enjoyable one. Bram was relieved to have been wrong about sharing the fact that the General had given him some reason to expect trouble. He went to be hoping that the General was wrong to be concerned and that his folks assigned to protect him would relax and enjoy the vacation.

Chapter 10: Highway Six

The next morning, Matt met them outside of the Hotel and they began the rather long journey up highway six. They all agreed that their first stop was to get coffee and a morning snack.

It was clear to Bram that his bodyguards had resumed their guarding roles when they walked through the entire coffee shop before sitting down for their coffee. Even then one of them stood near the door in a relaxed position until replaced by one of the others.

He knew that the routine would continue wherever they stopped. This was what he had wanted to keep from happening, but he knew that given the past history of all the attacks they had experienced, the attack would occur when they least expected.

The drive-up highway six soon left civilization behind and nestled itself along the valleys that seemed to serve as passageways between the snowcapped mountains. Bram quietly took in the forest trees that seemed to form a gauntlet of various shades of green that had a soaring clear blue hood that seemed to have no end.

He thought that the sun's streaming rays seemed to be emitted from a glittering disco ball and belied the fact that somewhere ahead the black rays of hate might change that beauty into the vengeful rain cast on them by Od, the mad avenging Norse god. He likened it to the Ying and Yang of good and evil. He felt the presence of all the old warriors and mythical gods of the Vikings.

By lunch time the peaceful and relaxing ride had them at Donbas.

There they selected a tavern that Bram commented meant Musk Ox Tavern in Norwegian and that was offering Elgburger, that meant Elk Burger as their lunch special.

They all got a laugh out of the fact that it was a Musk Ox Tavern that had a special featuring Elk versus Musk Ox.

Zoe said that the restaurant owner must have gotten the idea by watching American Football where cows were recommending that folks eat more chicken.

The waitress suggested they try the Hubertus liqueur drink that was featured as a special to go with the meal. She explained that St. Hubertus was the patron of hunters, and that the bartender had a secret mix that people raved about because it was light and refreshing.

They all ordered it and later agreed that it had been a great drink recommendation.

After lunch, the drive continued to Trondheim. The plan was to stay there for the night. It was a pleasant drive with pine covered mountains on both sides.

They drove along the banks of several long lakes that made it look like the mountains and sky went up into the sky and also went deep down into the lake. They stopped at a high point and got out and stood and embraced the scene with their eyes and mind. They all stood in silence for a few moments absorbing the mesmeric beauty.

Zoe commented that it was hard to get back into the van and leave such splendor behind.

They arrived at just the right time at the Trol restaurant where the set menu featured clam on the half shell, Trondheimssodd, soup, or Sodd, diced mutton meat balls, and a side of Norwegian flatbread. They all ordered Stjørdalsøl beer with the meal and a Karsk, coffee and moonshine, with desert.

They agreed that the menu had been very different than they expected and the coffee with moonshine had ensured they would get a good night's sleep.

After the meal they agreed to a walk before checking in to the hotel.

They followed Melisa's suggestion and made breakfast reservations for eight in the morning.

The hotel desk clerk asked for them to select their breakfast items so the kitchen could have them ready for such an early breakfast time.

The next morning after a leisurely breakfast, they again followed Melisa's suggestion, stopped at a local grocery, and stocked up on snacks so they could last and have a late lunch when they got to Grong.

It was a long but enjoyable ride. The drinks and snacks were exactly what they needed.

In Grong they stopped and did pizza and then continued their drive to Fauske.

They arrived in Fauske and decided on dinner before checking in. The recommendation was to eat at the Orlando Bar and Grill. They all felt that it was appropriate because of their close friendship with Orlando. They decided that each of them would order a different item from the menu so they could get an overall impression of the place.

They got one order of Orlando's House Steak that, based on its size, they were sure was meant for a family of four, an order of ribs that was served on a large board and had onion rings heaped on it and a side salad, another similar order that had slices of beef, sweet potato fries and what seemed to be mac and cheese but with a different taste and one slab of ribs and fries made the final item.

A pitcher of golden Kroonenberg lager beer was ordered for the table.

The discussion focused on how good everything was and how enjoyable the ride had been so far.

Fold Wormhole

They asked for a copy of the menu so they could send it back to Orlando as a souvenir.

After Dinner they checked in at the hotel and made their breakfast reservations.

The next morning after breakfast they piled in and headed toward Bjerkvik where they planned to have a late lunch and perhaps chose to spend the night.

They had agreed that their desired goal was to get to Bardufoss out on highway Eighty-Six that had a large barn that could serve as a Fold receive-transmit site.

Matt let them know that there would be a ferry ride from Bognes to a point were highway six continued in a valley on the other side of a range of mountains.

They got to Bognes, where they had to wait for the arrival of the ferry. They went into the coffee shop and had a coffee and an ice cream cone.

They were all outside walking along a path that led to the water when Pat pointed out the arrival of the ferry.

Matt led the way back to the van. He got the van in line leading to the ferry loading dock.

A truck cut in front of them, and Zoe commented about the rudeness of the driver of the truck. It seemed to strike a nerve.

The loader for the ferry signaled the truck to come onto the ferry first and positioned it up at the bow of the barge. He positioned cars around and behind the van.

The loader then positioned their van behind the truck. He seemed to be balancing the load so that the ferry would be level.

There was an announcement letting folks know how long the transit would be and that there were refreshments for sale on the enclosed viewing deck.

As soon as the van was in position and turned off, Zoe jumped out and signaled Thomas to follow her. She asked Eric to take Bram to the side behind the shielded part of the ferry.

She told Bob to stay and get ready for action.

Pat immediately had her radar at full power. She knew that Zoe was in the attack mode. She was not sure what had triggered Zoe, but she trusted Zoe's instincts.

Zoe followed the two men that had gotten out of the truck up to the viewing deck. She positioned Thomas on one side of the viewing deck, and she went to the other side. She was not sure what she was expecting but her senses were tingling. She moved in slowly toward the driver of the truck. He seemed pre-occupied as if waiting for something to happen.

The ferry pulled slowly away from the pier and then smoothly turned its bow in the direction they were going. The water was calm, and the ferry had only a gentle sway as it cut through the water. It was under way for about twenty minutes when there was a thunderous explosion. The nose of the ferry lifted up and then the nose seemed to take a dive down.

Fold Wormhole

A horn started blaring and the boat seemed to stop and then the entire ferry trembled as the engines seemed to groan and begin a laborious pull backwards. The nose seemed to slowly come back up to the surface like a person who had fallen try to push themselves up.

Zoe called Eric and told him to push the truck off the ferry. At the same time, she pulled her gun and shot the driver of the truck in the head as he lifted his hand with a control pad in it. She took a quick step forward and deftly caught the control that was blinking in midair.

The bullet in the brain had shut down the signal to the finger about to push the button.

The controls in her hand was still active.

She heard Thomas shoot three times and knew that that the second person in the truck was dead. She kept her mind on the controller in her hand.

She felt the front of the boat rise higher and knew that the truck had been pushed over the edge.

She counted slowly to twenty and then pressed the button.

She had not been prepared for the size of the explosion and was thrown off her feet. She stood up and rushed to the window and saw the water that had been blown up into the air as if fell back down. She was surprised to see a ten-foot wave heading toward the ferry.

She called Eric and told him to get ready to withstand the wave.

The Captain had turned the ferry to a forty-five-degree angle as the wave caught up to it.

Eric pushed everyone behind the van. It seemed to be a reasonable place.

The water swept over the car deck and almost took Matt over the side. Bram reached out and pulled him back behind the van.

The front of the Ferry slowly rose out of the water and the ferry turned and the wave caught it on its side and pushed it along.

The Captain expertly guided the ferry, so that it turned and slid sidewards down the other side of the wave.

It was clear to Zoe that they were lucky to have someone at the helm that seemed to know how to handle the ferry.

Everyone in the viewing deck was flat on the floor. Zoe pulled out her badge and declared that she and Thomas were taking charge of the ferry.

She climbed up to where the captain was steering the ferry backwards toward shore and asked him whether he could make it to the other end of the journey.

He asked who she was, shook his head saying it didn't matter. He replied that he felt that he could but was heading in as close to shore as he dared just in case he had to off load the people. He then asked who she had shot with the gun she was holding.

Zoe holstered her weapon and said it was the driver of the truck bomb and his accomplice were both dead on the viewing deck. Everyone else was fine.

Fold Wormhole

Out on the car deck, Matt had taken out his sophisticated rocket grenade launcher and was trying to get a sense of where the rocket that had hit the ferry had originated. He knew that he only had to get the approximate location and then the smart flying grenade would follow it's sensors to the target.

Bram reached into the back of the van and pulled out the weapon that looked like an AR 15 but was slightly different.

Matt pointed to the safety of the rifle.

Bram looked up just in time to see a low flying drone coming in just above the water surface. Without saying a word, he began to put out a stream of bullets in front of the drone in hopes that he would be able to put enough shrapnel in front of it to take it out.

Another explosion out to the front of the ferry almost knocked him down but he continued to fire at the incoming drone.

He saw the wave wash over the ferry and grabbed Matt and pulled him behind the van to keep him from being swept overboard.

The drone exploded a few hundred feet from the ferry and knocked both of them down. The van shook and one side of it was lifted by the force and the side panel could be heard crunching.

He recovered to see a second drone and was going to fire, but his weapon was empty. He felt Pat's hand on his shoulder as she handed him another cannister of bullets. He quickly removed the empty cannister and snapped in the full one. He then proceeded to fill the sky with lead.

Once again he was blown back into the van as the drone blew up.

Matt had repeatedly fired his flying grenades and was just getting back on his feet when three jets streaked in and lit up the mountain side with a series of rockets.

A mushroom cloud rose up from the area and for a few moments blocked out the sun.

The jets were followed by three Marine helicopters that could be seen coming in low and heading toward the point where the rockets had hit.

The ferry, now traveling backwards but staying afloat headed on to the landing dock. Once they were almost to the dock, the ferry captain turned the ferry and ran it full throttle up the ramp that was to the side of the off-loading dock.

He came on the loudspeaker and said that the authorities were on the way and that everyone would off load when cleared by them.

He announced that all refreshments were free.

He informed the passengers that when the vehicles were off loaded, they would be able to travel on after the authorities cleared them.

He then turned to Zoe and thanked her for having taken action against the attackers and then being generous enough to have paid for the refreshments. He was not sure how his boat would be repaired. It was his private ferry, but he said that having it up on the ramp was a miracle and he would worry about repair once he got over having survived.

Zoe followed the captain as he pointed out the damage at the front of the barge. He commented that the steel bulkhead with its doors closed had prevented the ferry from sinking

She gave him an address and suggested he get the repair done and send the bill and ask for reimbursement. She told him to refer to the Fold organization.

When the authorities arrived, they asked for Bram and then took them all aside and informed them that they had gotten clearance to go on from the very top of the Norwegian government. They were cleared to leave at any time. He suggested they get away from the scene in case there were more terrorists around.

Matt led them out to where the van was parked. He pointed to the passenger's side of the van and the place where Bram had been blown twice into it and commented that he thought that two Bram butt prints was the only damage the van had sustained. He shook his head and asked how Bram was feeling.

Bram suggested that Matt ask him the following day because he knew that he was still on an adrenalin high.

Matt asked Zoe how she had known that an attack was going to happen.

Zoe replied that she hadn't known but her senses had tingled, and she had acted.

Matt told her to let him know the next time that she felt that way.

They had been driving for about an hour when Matt commented that they were about to enter a tunnel that was almost a mile long.

They entered the brightly lit tunnel when Zoe sitting turned to look back at the entrance and saw a large truck come up from a side road and get behind them. She called out for Matt to floor it and go as fast as he could and if anything got in his way to go around it. She told him not to let anything stop him because she was sure it was a trap.

He floored it and took the van past the hundred mile per hour mark. He spotted a truck, ahead of them, taking up the middle of the road in front of him and knew he was in trouble.

He hesitated for a moment when he felt a foot press down on his gas pedal foot.

Thomas yelled to make it fit.

He yelled for everyone to hold on as he passed the truck and both sides of the van scrapped. The metal siding ripping of the driver's side sounded like the crunching of a car crusher in a junk yard. The sparks seemed to engulf the van.

Fold Wormhole

Matt guided the van past the truck and kept the pedal flat to the floor as he tried to regain speed. The blue sky at the end of the tunnel seem to beckon but not get any closer. Matt kept muttering come on, come on.

Zoe looked back and saw the truck gaining on them. She climbed over her seat, used the cargo net to secure herself and opened the back door of the van. She began firing her weapon at the truck. She shot the radiator and the tires until she had emptied her weapon.

Eric handed her, his weapon when she emptied hers.

She kept on firing. She had the radiator steaming but the truck was still gaining.

Eric then handed her reloaded weapon back to her and she concentrated on the driver of the truck. The wind shiel of the truck shattered and she hit the driver at least three times.

Suddenly, the truck swerved and blocked the entire tunnel as it slid sidewards, still gaining on them, and then exploded.

The van seemed to get a push from behind like the next stage of a rocket launch as the explosion sent a shock wave out of the tunnel.

They were in the clear. Eric helped Zoe back across the back seat as Matt brought the van to a stop.

Matt got out of the van and looked over the damage that had been absorbed. He tried the crumpled and bent back doors and concluded they would not open. The force of the explosion had bent them, and they no longer were functional.

The rest of them got out and after looking at the collapsed rubble that had been the tunnel opening, they walked around the van.

The entire frame on the left side of the van was exposed. The metal bullet proof armor was still in place, but it looked like a picture from one of the science fiction Borg movies. The right side of the van had a flattened exterior, but it was still in place.

Matt commented that he was surprised that the bullet proof glass had withstood the various impacts.

He said that he checked off one miracle for having survived the ferry and now he checked off number two miracle, for having escaped the trap and having survived.

He thanked Thomas for having given his foot an offer it could not refuse.

Zoe asked if there were any more tunnels and if there were he should take the long way around.

He asked if anyone objected to driving straight through to Bardufoss to the farmhouse that was the final destination in Norway.

There were no objections.

Highway six had more tunnels but each time Matt took the old and slightly longer way around that took them along the coast.

He got no objections to taking the slightly longer ways along the coast.

They arrived to Bardufoss late in the afternoon and drove out to the farmhouse that Melisa had purchased.

They had not eaten since before getting on the ferry and were ready to go out before settling in for the night.

The restaurant that seemed to have the best menu was a Thai restaurant. They ordered sushi and egg rolls as starters then everyone ordered their choices off the menu.

Zoe was complimented for taking the lead in foiling the attacks that had occurred.

Bram commented that it was OK for her to tweak his nose in the future.

Zoe laughed and said that she had been so thrilled by all the adventure that Bram provided that tweaking his nose no longer interested her, but she wanted to go on vacation with him more often.

Matt said that he would warn other Marine's about getting assigned to escort the Bram group. He was going to report back to Orlando that he had just experienced more battle action acting as a driver than their unit had shared in Iraq.

Pat nodded and asked what they thought it was like living with Bram. She had yet to decide what a normal life with him might be. Anytime Bram took off from work, it always ended up with some short of fireworks. She commented that the last Fourth of July as they watched the fireworks she realized they were having a quiet night out.

Zoe added that she now swam in short shorts and wore a solid halter top just in case she had to jump any fences to save Bram.

Bram shook his head and said they were exaggerating and that there were quiet moments.

Eric nodded and said that there were many quiet moments if they could count the hours from ten at night until five in the morning as moments but otherwise, outings with him seemed to be times to make sure your weapon didn't jam.

Bob and Thomas both lifted their beers and said, "hear, hear."

Chapter 11: Finland

In Helsinki, Melisa had purchased the entire sixth floor of a building in the center of the city. The apartment had one bedroom designated as the Fold arrival and departure room.

She had arranged for a day tour by private car. The tour guide was to meet them outside of the apartment building and would first take them to a restaurant of their choice.

The Fold in was flawless but a surprise awaited them.

Once again Zoe led the way for a sweep of the apartment before allowing Bram out of the Fold arrival-departure room. She called back that she had apprehended an intruder and was holding him in the living room and that Bram should come and verify who he was.

Bram knew that Zoe would never have called for him if there was any risk. He was, however, surprised by finding General Tilson with his hands up in the air but smiling.

The General smiled and said he had come to complain. He said that he was complaining about the fact that Bram and his FBI team had usurped the protective role of the young Marine with whom he had chatted this morning. This young Marine had complained that the action was usurped by Bram and his team, and that he felt that the protection that he was supposed to provide instead resulted in him getting saved by the person he was to protect. This Marine said he was especially impressed with a gun totting, sharp shooting young FBI lady that took out a bomb laden truck as she risked falling out the back of the van he was driving. He figured out later that she had just been trying to save herself by having the shock wave from the resulting exploding truck fling her back into the van and slam the van doors shut. Doors that this Marine said would need to be replaced.

He claims to have been the weakest link in the Bram Nielson army and was saved from being swept overboard into the cold sea where he was certain to have died. He said that a hand grabbed his uniform and literally lifted him up and put him down against the back of the van as a wave swept the car next to it into the sea. That hand was not the hand of god but at that instant it was certainly guided by the mighty one.

Bram smiled and replied that this young Marine that the General was describing was a student of Orlando and was demonstrating the story telling lessons he had learned from the great storyteller that had mentored him.

Fold Wormhole

Bram emphasized that Sergeant Simple had the wrong rank and should be called Sergeant Major of the Marine Corps, SMMC, and also be made to wear the Marine great storyteller pin on his breast pocket and be recognized as a hard-core representative of the USMC.

He should also be commended with taking out the missile launch site that had scored a hit on the ferry and in driving like a mad man to get them out of the tunnel trap.

Bram said if the general didn't have a job for this Marine, he would make him an offer that would most likely be accepted.

The General gave a laugh and said that the young Marine indeed would be called Sergeant Major, and he would be in a role as an aid to a General that had caught the big cheese and who had turned down a DC assignment to stay with the Fold community.

Bram suggested they hear the rest of the story at dinner and rattled off twelve restaurants withing a ten-block radius. He made the point that the next big decision was to agree on which kind of cuisine they were interested in because the restaurants he had named featured Finish traditional to Vietnamese Phó and every cuisine in-between.

He suggested they avoid the Finish Traditional menu because he said that Melisa had arranged with the tour guide to take them to traditional restaurants during their day tour.

They decided to go with a restaurant that featured Italian cuisine.

They ordered several different items on the menu, and they agreed that they would share.

The final order consisted of Risotto Alla Milanese paired with Osso buco, a meat-based Lasagna, Spaghetti Alla Carbonara with guanciale, and two Neapolitan pizza variations as main dishes. They added Arancini, Sicilian rice balls, Eggplant Parmigiana, green beans, stuffed tomatoes, stuffed Artichokes, marinated mushrooms, and stuffed zucchini flowers as sides.

The waiter complimented them on the variety that had been ordered and said that soft Italian breadsticks would be out immediately with whatever drinks they ordered.

He let them know that there were three featured deserts that they might want to try: Lemon Ricotta Cake with Almonds, Tiramisu and Affogato, an Italian coffee-based desert.

Once the order was in, the General said that he had successfully identified the person that his Marine spy was informing. He was a recently retired Marine General that had been passed over and pushed out because of his behavior. He shared that he had personally recommended the ouster.

He described letting his small fish Marine take leave to go visit his family, but he was followed to Wyoming where the Marine General lived and seen going to his ranch.

The General shared that he had the NSA intercept the call from the ranch to a group in Norway, so I knew I had him.

I then assigned, Sergeant Simple to be the driver of a heavily bullet-proofed van that would carry you on the drive through Norway.

Had I known the fire power that was about to be used, I would have stopped the trip. It was a lesson that I will not forget. I underestimated the fire power that might be used.

I did arrange with my Navy Admiral friend to have an aircraft carrier doing an exercise along the coast and have them prepared to provide assistance if called for. I had a Marine Corps helicopter group assigned to the aircraft career.

When Sergeant Simple called for support and received both Navy and Marine support.

The Norwegian leadership at the very top were appraised, ahead of time, of the situation and agreed to clear the diplomatic way.

I learned from them about the attack in the tunnel when they informed me and shared that it was a miracle that the van had escaped. They let me know that the tunnel would be closed for at least six months.

He then shared that he had the Marine General being held in a Navy brig in San Diego. He planned to have all the nitty gritty detail of his traitorous actions exposed at his court martial. He was sure that at a minimum this General would get thirty years to life.

Zoe commented that she hoped it would be life. She said she wasn't vindictive, but she was amazed that a person that had spent his career in the military could end up so twisted in his mind that he was willing to support killing a person to settle a personal grievance.

General Tilson nodded, agreed, and said that in his mind execution would be more appropriate.

A second round of drinks were ordered as the meal was served.

Pat guided the discussion to the tour they planned to take on the following day.

Hours later the dinner ended with everyone sharing a little of each of the three desert specials.

During the walk back, the General said that he was Folding back to Dallas where it was now midnight. He planned to get things rolling and have Sergeant Simple promoted and transferred to be his aid.

The next morning, they went down and were greeted by the tour guide as they reached the street. She was a young lady that introduced herself as Anneli and her driver as Eetu. She gave a brief introduction of her qualifications and said that she had been giving tours for five years while she attended the University of Helsinki where she was about to graduate with a master's degree. She added that Eetu was also a student there.

She escorted them into the restaurant and helped them put in their breakfast order. She let them know that she had already had breakfast and would settle for a cup of coffee.

Bram asked what her degree was in.

Anneli said that her degree was in science and that she had focused on studying elementary particles, the development of the solar system, the stars, and galaxies. She said that the curriculum fulfilled the requirements for her degree. She felt that she had gotten an extensive understanding of these areas. She hoped to be able to land a job that would allow her to dig even deeper into one of these areas.

Bram asked how she was doing in her class.

She responded that she was trying hard, but she was coming out number three in her class and being out done by two very smart people. She said that she was in the last stage of her battle and planned to win.

Pat expected Bram to give the young lady his card but when he didn't, she knew that he was going to wait to see how she led the tour. She hoped that Anneli carried herself well during the tour.

Pat knew how it was to try and be on the top of the pecking order. She had fought very hard to earn the top spot on in her astronaut class. She had felt very lucky to have been supported by Amy who had been the number two in the class and who had a direct connection to Bram.

It had been a total surprise to have risen from number three in the class and have taken the top spot. She understood the emotionally tough one had to be. She had lived the situation.

Pat knew that Bram had a keen ability to evaluate a person and know how they might fit into the Fold program. He was on the hunt for more brain power. So Pat was going to do everything possible to give Anneli the opportunity to show her ability.

Throughout the tour Pat asked questions about the history of a statue or the history of a building or an institution. She was pleased that Anneli would admit when she did not know an answer but replied that she would find out the answer before the end of the tour.

She watched to see if Bram had any reaction but knew he would not show any.

The first part of the tour ended when Anneli suggested they have lunch at a famous Finnish restaurant known for its traditional menu items. She said the food was superb and the view enchanting, but she warned that it was one of the more expensive restaurants in the city.

Zoe said she was all for it since the bill would be going to Bram.

Anneli called ahead to make the reservations and then shared that the restaurant wanted to let them know that the tip for a group their size was twenty percent.

Fold Wormhole

This time Pat spoke up and said that she hoped the service and food lived up to Anneli's description.

They were greeted at the door and immediately made to feel as if they were important customers. They were offered a tour of both levels of the dining area. The place was crowded, and Pat commented that the aroma of food was making her hungry.

They were led to a table on the second level that had a splendid view of the harbor.

They discussed how to order. The waiter highlighted the available specials and said there were also set menus.

Pat had made sure to let Anneli know that she and Eetu were to join them for lunch. She immediately liked the way that Anneli at first said that she shouldn't, but it was so hard to say no. She said that she had always wanted eat there but had never been able to bring herself to spent that amount of money.

Pat gave a small laugh and said that it was on the budget, and she should enjoy herself.

Pat asked Bram what he was thinking about ordering.

He replied that he was going for the grilled scallops, rainbow trout roe, truffle, and the celery consommé.

Pat asked if they could share and said she would order the Pelmeni, mushrooms and the mushroom consommé.

Zoe was making a similar bargain with Eric and said that she was going for the pan-fried grouse, the goose liver, celery, and the hunter's sauce.

For desert they decided to order baked Alaska.

After all the lunch orders were in they discussed what type of wine they should order. They settled on ordering one bottle of Inniskillin Gold Vidal Ice wine that claimed to have a mouthwatering spicy apricot finish and a bottle of wine made from bilberry, a bottle of Artic bramble, and a bottle of white currant wine.

They ended up spending almost two hours for lunch as they each tried a little of everything.

Anneli said they should not worry about running out of time. She planned to make sure they got the full treatment and that she would end the tour outside of another great restaurant.

Anneli did a great job of taking them to a location getting them out for a quick walk around as she described the history of the area and then getting them to the next location. She kept up a swift pace but thoroughly described what they were seeing.

The evening arrived but because of the time of year, the night did not darken, and it seemed like only late afternoon.

Bob commented about feeling like it was early but said that his body told him it was time to eat again.

The menu once again had a great variety to choose from that was unique and delicious. They continued their adventure into the northern ice wines and unique deserts.

As the dinner came to a close, Bram finally handed Anneli his business card and suggested she send him her resume when it was time for her to graduate.

Fold Wormhole

He let her know that she would experience the universe like she had never imagined, and it would be much better than the two superb meals that she had just eaten.

Anneli commented that it sounded too good to be true, but she would definitely send her resume.

Bram's card had the word FOLD in red on a dark blue background and his snail mail address and his e-mail address of BramNielson37@gmail.com.

Anneli looked at the card and said that she liked its simplicity, and she would send her resume as soon as she got it written.

Pat hoped that she would and do it as early as possible. Pat knew it would be a once in a lifetime opportunity.

When they got back to the apartment, they decided to Fold to Stockholm so that they could have an early start the next day.

The apartment in Stockholm was similar in size to the others that they had used. It was on the top floor, and they later learned that it took up one quarter of the building it was in.

The arrival routine was followed, and they were soon moving into their rooms, showering, and heading for bed.

The next morning, they went out and walked the large square that was adjacent to the apartment. There were several restaurants, but none opened early except a Burger Shop. They decided to walk to a nearby bakery that featured a variety of sweet rolls, bread and a large selection of cheese and sausage.

Bram mentioned that they would have two large Swedish meals, and that Melisa had instructed their guide to take them to restaurants that served traditional Swedish Food.

Pat called the guide and let him know where to pick them up. The guide introduced herself as Elena and she introduced the driver as her partner Milind. She made the point that both of them were professional tour guides that had gone to a special school that focused on educating them in the history of Sweden and of Stockholm. She shared that the two of them took turns being in charge, but they were business partners.

She went on to say that the two had toured, a Melisa Etrius, who had set up the tour they were about to experience. She smiled and said that Melisa had been very specific about the tour being paced so that the main highlights of Stockholm would be visited and that the best restaurants enjoyed.

Elena then rattled off the land-oriented sites of the 13th-century Storkyrkan Cathedral, the Kungliga Slottet Royal Palace, and that the last place would be the Nobel Museum, which focuses on the Nobel Prize.

She said that she would have a running commentary about all the historic buildings they would drive by, but she did not expect them to remember them but said that a video of the highlights of the entire tour was part of the package.

Then they would stop for a traditional lunch at a top restaurant that had a view of the bay.

Lunch would be a traditional Swedish lunch.

Fold Wormhole

For the Main they would have the choice of,

Grilled Falukorv, a beef and pork sausage served with creamy
            macaroni, Smörgåstårta, Sweden's number one meal
            where everything is put on bread, in layers, and
            serve it as a cake.

Korv, a Swedish Sausage Stroganoff with a bowl of steaming rice.

The table would be graced with a generous number of sides.

    Julskinka ham
    Wallenbergare – Veal Patties
    Swedish Lingonberry Sauce
    Raggmunk – Swedish Potato Pancakes
    Hasselbackspotatis – Swedish Hasselback, spiral cut potatoes
    Gubbröra – Egg And Anchovy Salad
    Semla – Swedish Sweet Buns
    Lussekatter – Saffron Buns

And then the desert selection would be.

    Ostkaka – Swedish Cheesecake
    Kladdkaka – Mud Cake
    Prinsesstårta – Princess Cake

She stopped and asked if they had any questions.

Thomas asked what the possibility was to just go straight to the restaurant and begin eating because the choices seemed overwhelming.

Zoe asked if they could discuss the menu and see what they would do for lunch and still have room for a dinner in the evening.

Elena laughed and said that they would be having the evening meal after a ferry ride to Fjäderholmen and eat at their most well-known restaurant and be sitting right at the edge of the water.

There they would focus on

Gravlax Dill, which was cured Salmon, served with cold potato and even more dill.

Sill, pickled herring, and fried herring

Räkmacka, which was an open-faced shrimp sandwich with complimentary toppings that included lettuce, mayonnaise, egg, dill, and caviar

Kräftor, which was local crayfish that had been boiled and then served cold laying over an ice bed.

She suggested that it would be the time to enjoy the evening and drink great Swedish beer such as Norrlands Guld, Falcon pale lager, or Närke Kaggen Stormaktsporter that had a twelve percent alcohol level.

She pointed out that it was also a time to choose to try one of the many fruit wines or ciders.

Eric commented that he was joining Thomas in the request to skip the tour and just get to the restaurants.

Milind looked at Elena and commented that she was glad to be driving because it was clear to her they had a group that was going to be tough to impress with old buildings and walks inside of museums.

Bram joined in and commented that they should try working with such a group. He smiled, shook his head, and pointed at each of team and then said that it was time to tour.

The morning tour went smoothly and when lunch time arrived, they indeed enjoyed a delicious meal with a variety of tastes that were new to them.

They shared a variety of beers and wines, and the deserts topped off the meal.

Fold Wormhole

Elena led them along the waterfront to where the Ferry was loading. She walked up to the gang plank and handed over the tickets and led them aboard.

They sat on the top deck where she handed out headsets and said that the ships tour guide would narrate the tour. They would first go along the center city side of the waterway and then they would turn and go close to the other side as they made their way to the island of Fjäderholmen. The journey was about ten miles out to the island. For much of the way Elena shared the history of Sweden and the Vikings.

Once on the Island, Elena led the way to the restaurant where a table had been set up and was waiting for them.

The waiter took their drink menu and shortly after the Hors d'oeuvre and the starters were brought out and they all got into the food as Elena described that food that was to be served.

Pat made sure that Elena and Milind were included in the meal.

They both thanked her for including them.

The sun was not in the sky, but the evening remained light and, on the ride back they enjoyed a darker view of the distant shoreline and as they approached the city, the lights seemed to sparkle.

The ride back to their apartment from the waterfront only took minutes. They thanked Elena and Milind for a great tour and said they would recommend them to their friends back in the states.

Pat handed each an envelope that held a generous tip before taking the elevator up to their apartment.

They spent a few moments checking what time it was in Dallas. Dallas was nine hours earlier than Stockholm. It was near ten in the evening, which they figured made it one in the afternoon in Dallas.

He and Pat had agreed to Fold to Rome at a later date. They both had enough of touring and were more interested in getting a good night's sleep in their own bed.

Bram suggested they all Fold back at midnight and arrive in Dallas in the afternoon. They would be able to have a late dinner and get a good night's sleep back in their own beds.

Zoe commented that she was looking forward to feeling safe in their armored home.

Chapter 12: Oversight

As the Fold back to Dallas materialized in the hanger, Bram saw that the General, and his new aid Matt and Linda were there to greet them.

The General greeted them, pointed to Matt's insignia, and said that his new aid should be addressed as Sergeant Major.

The team congratulated Matt and said that he deserved the promotion.

Matt thanked them and then commented that he could not believe what he was learning about the Fold program.

He said that he had spent a great amount of time talking to his buddy, now also a Sergeant Major but a guy that soon would hold the rank of an officer, about all the things that was going on in the Fold program. It all seemed to be surreal and seemed to be a story out of a science fiction book.

Bram smiled and said that he often felt the same way.

Linda greeted them and let Bram know that she had been fending off the leader of the Oversight committee who was insisting that the committee take a tour of the facility and get an understanding of the work that was going on. He wanted to examine the spending records and wanted to be shown where the money had been spent. She said that Jeffrey was on the committee as well and was the new head of the NASA organization. He had called her and shared that he was having a tough time with several committee members who seemed to think they knew a better way to manage the Fold program.

She let him know that Jeffrey was the first thing on his agenda on his first morning at work. She wanted to know what morning that would be.

Bram replied that he would be in on Monday and then he wanted to review all the work that had gone on with each of the team leaders before meeting with Jeffrey.

He also asked Linda to work with Zoe to verify that all the members on the Oversight committee had the proper level of clearance.

He then signaled for Castor to lead the way to the transport van.

Once they got to the house, they all gathered in his office, and he shared the fact that he was planning to move much of the work being done in Dallas to Einstein City on Mataia, but they would personally remain very visible during the workday in the Dallas facility.

Fold Wormhole

The records he was going to give the committee would be extensive. It would be almost impossible for the committee to get anything useful from the records, but he hoped that they would spend their time trying to understand them.

He asked that his office get checked several times a day for listening devices, as well as video devices. He also wanted the perimeter of the office building checked for any parked vans or other vehicles that might house listening devices.

He made a point that he wanted the whole house checked and then he asked for a random check any time the house was unoccupied.

He said he was sure that an attempt would be made to compromise their communications. He asked that each member of the committee have their background scrutinized. He wanted to know every detail of what the members had ever done.

Zoe commented that the committee members had better be squeaky clean or they were toast. She was going to have a friend of hers check for anything that would disqualify the member.

Bram asked that she co-ordinate with Linda so that wires would not get crossed.

The next day, Pat invited Mallica, Remi, Melisa, and Marcus and his two kids to Sunday breakfast. She knew that Bram would take the opportunity to get back into the rhythm of his work. She figured that the breakfast would be a great way to allow him to do it.

Bram thanked her and said that he would prepare the morning meal.

Thomas heard the exchange and said that according to his calculations it was his turn to do the cooking, and he planned to do so.

Bram knew that was not the case and knew that it was his turn, but he appreciated Thomas's offer and thanked him.

The offer made Bram think about the role his bodyguards had played in the encounter in Norway. He went down to his office and documented what the four of them had done.

He asked the four to review what he had written.

Eric and Zoe both commented that he was making them all sound like heroes that had survived a perilous battle.

Bram replied that it indeed was a dangerous situation that the four of them handled exceptionally well.

He checked with both Bob and Thomas who each expressed a similar view that Bram was being very generous in his praise.

Bram then sent the document to their FBI boss first thanking him for assigning the cream of the cream to guard him and made the suggestion that the four get promoted and get financially rewarded.

Pat had come in and had caught the gist of what the report said. She commented that she wanted to be rewarded as well.

Bram gave a laugh and asked what she was currently getting paid. He said that her boss ought to at least double whatever that might be since she had to put up with him twenty-four, seven.

He did not know what her current salary was because Erica managed the personnel files of everyone in the Fold organization.

He sent a quick note to Erica suggesting that both Pat and Amy get raises to reward the work they had done in setting up Einstein City.

While he was at it he sent Jeffrey a note recommending a raise for Erica to reward her outstanding management of the Fold organization.

After making sure those who constantly had his back were rewarded, he felt good and suggested that they take a walk around the neighborhood.

He let Pat know that he was now into thinking about the beings from the Water World. He was wondering how they were doing. He said he was eager to hear from Mallica and Gerry who were leading the effort to get the Swoshians transitioning to a new Water World.

He then brought up the topic of the production of the additional vessels that the Swoshians would use to make the transition. He knew that Erika and Remi would be on top of that.

He wanted to catch up with Marcus on what he had found out about negative Fold space as well as the continued effort in the normal Fold space.

He gave a small laugh as he then highlighted the work that Remi was doing.

Then he looked at Pat and said that he wondered about Amy's progress in getting Einstein City completed and ready for use.

Pat smiled and said that she was sure Amy had made great progress, but the city would need tweaking and adjustment as they moved in and identified the things that had been missed.

She made the point that Bram had too many irons in the fire.

She highlighted additional irons; how Zuri and Orlando were doing in their studies, how Lacy was doing with her protection offense, and what Melisa's progress in setting up the around the world Fold vacation spots happened to be.

Bram agreed that there were many irons in the fire and that they needed to organize the work in such a fashion that the new oversight committee would not impede the progress that they were making.

Pat suggested that they use honey to distract the committee. Bram asked what she had in mind.

Pat pointed out that the committee members would want to understand the Fold technology. Having them experience it would give Bram the opportunity to influence each of the members. She suggested that they do a survey of the committee members and determine what their favorite vacation spot in the world might be and then accompany them in the Fold weekend mini-vacation experience to that spot.

Fold Wormhole

They needed to make sure that Melinda had vetted the desired location and set it up for a Fold vacation but other than that they could keep the members busy for quite a while as they all experienced a Fold vacation. She bet that afterwards the committee would be much more supportive of the work that was going on.

Bram agreed that Pat had hit on a terrific way to make the committee much easier to work with.

The breakfast was into full swing on Sunday morning when Erica and Gerry walked in. She looked around the table and saw that General Tilson and his new attaché Matt were also in attendance. After greeting everyone she looked at Bram and asked if it was a business meeting.

Bram nodded and said that he wanted to get ready for the coming week so that he would know how he would manage the oversight committee. He pointed out that he just wanted the top line of where everyone was and that the details could be held until the regular work week.

He looked over at Melisa and said he wanted to begin with understanding how the Fold tourist agency was doing.

Melissa said the Fold tourist agency was overwhelmed with the requests it had received. She had limited the weekend vacation departures from Friday afternoon until Saturday morning. She thanked Remi for making the dozen or so bubbles available.

She said that a bubble had gone out every ten minutes during the eight hours that she operated the weekend schedule. The feedback was off the charts and positive. She had made the charges seventy per cent of what a normal hotel reservations were. Food and entertainment were not included.

She said that the Fold could be automated but so far she had personally managed the Folds. She had wanted to ensure that no one got stuck in any of the locations. She said that everyone in the room had availed themselves of the vacation opportunity and that the best feedback she had received was that from Marcus Jr and Mylan who had made three weekend outings with Marcus.

Bram asked Mylan where they had gone. She said they had gone to Tokyo Japan, taken a bullet train to Mt Fuji, had visited the Imperial Palace and Shinjuku Gyoen National Garden. She said that they had eaten only traditional Japanese meals and loved them.

Marcus Jr. said that Australia had been great. It was like visiting the US, but the accent of the people there made it so much fun to talk to them when they met along the beach. He said that his favorite food had been the Lamingtons cake, which was a moist mouthwatering, butter sponge cake dipped in chocolate and coated with coconut.

Elizabeth commented that she loved Lamingtons cake and would bring one the next time they had a dinner at Bram's place.

Fold Wormhole

Marcus volunteered that the New Zealand weekend had been his selection. There they went up the ten-thousand-foot Sky Tower and got a spectacular view across the city and the area around it as far as the eye could see.

He said that he had considered bungee jumping and sky diving but figured that with his luck the bungee cord would snap, and the sky dive parachute would fail to open and he smashing into the ground. So, he settled for a city bus tour and a walk on the beach.

He said that the truly unique experience was a meal of Hāngi the traditional Māori way of cooking, where food is cooked in a covered pit lined with hot stones and fire. There was an assortment of meat and vegetables wrapped in flax leaves and the food was amazingly tender and delicious.

He laughed and said that the other favorite was the Hokey pokey ice cream consisting of vanilla-flavored ice cream with small lumps of honeycomb toffee dispersed throughout it.

He added that the weekend mini vacations helped the three of them focus on getting their work done during the week so they could enjoy the weekend. It had been a great way to continue their bonding and getting over not having Myla around.

Erica volunteered that she and Gerry had visited three Islands, the Falklands, Palermo Sicily, and Cyprus. The beaches had been the focus of their stay in each, but they had enjoyed the local cuisine in both Sicily and Cyprus.

Lacy said that she and Ray had also taken advantage of doing weekend mini vacations. They had stayed in country and had gone to three National parks.

They had not camped out but had gone on day hikes and enjoyed the homes that Melisa had purchased. They had enjoyed the local foods that consisted mostly of steak or ribs fixed in very unique and delicious ways.

Mallica joined in and said she had Folded to the Orlando's apartment in Oxford three times and enjoyed weekends with he and Zuri. She said that they mostly ate, Italian, Chinese, and French cuisine but also cooked in.

She said that the weekend Fold cycle let her romance with Orlando stay fresh.

Linda then said that she too had taken advantage of the Fold mini vacation and had gone to Alaska, Cozumel, and Jamaica. She complemented Melisa in having discovered and set up the locations so that the arrival and departures were invisible to the local population.

General Tilson had been quietly observing the interaction of the people that he knew were closest to Bram. He was impressed with their dedication and their ability to independently make their own decisions and take action.

He spoke up and said he would share how he had used the bubble to help catch the big cheese he had been after. He said that he worked with Marcus, Remi, and Lacy.

Fold Wormhole

He Folded to multiple locations that included Oxford where he had engaged Orlando and identified Matt as the person to provide the vacation protection for Bram and the rest of the team.

He had also visited the Admiral and personally gotten him to help in providing additional Navy support.

He admitted that he had underestimated and had been surprised by the ability of his adversary to mount multiple substantial attacks with the armament that had been used. He found it hard to envision that a military officer of his rank would to be willing to jeopardize the good of his country over a private game of revenge against him.

He then highlighted how impressed he was with the FBI body guards that took out two terrorists and prevented a truck bomb from being blown up on the ferry that had already been hit by a kamikaze drone.

He then related Matt's story about Bram shooting down two kamikaze drones while at the same time saving him from being washed overboard.

Bram spoke up and said that Matt had taken out the kamikaze launch site and later had driven like a mad man to save all of them from another truck bomb that had been positioned in a long underground tunnel as a barrier.

He recounted how Matt had propelled the van between the semitruck and the tunnel wall. He pointed out that because Matt had literally squeezed a size ten van through a size six car space they were all present to enjoy breakfast.

Matt said that he had not expected the van to make it through but an extra foot on top of his had not given him a choice and that afterward it was clear to him that the truck was going to be able to catch them, but Zoe willingly risked falling out of the back of the van to take out the driver of the truck. The truck crashed, exploded and he literally had to steer a van flying through the air. He was relieved to have watched the back doors of the van slam shut and Zoe climb back into her seat.

He said that he never expected to get the opportunity to learn why Bram and his team needed him to protect them but since he had arrived in the Dallas Fold compound, he had been exposed to so much new technology and wonder that he was finding it hard to absorb it all. He had no idea that such technology existed. He said that his ride back with the General had been so amazing that he still wondered if it all was real.

He smiled and said that the famous pancakes, smothered in Maple syrup helped him appreciate the taste of reality as it existed in the new environment that he was trying to absorb.

Bram acknowledged that Pat's famous pancakes always brought him to reality as well.

He then asked Amy how the work at Einstein City was going.

Amy replied that everything was ready.

She highlighted the fact that Remi was spending several hours each day making sure the lab facility was up and functioning.

Fold Wormhole

She had recruited Linh and Duong to set up the computer systems and she reminded Bram of the old Electrician that had made sure the electrical wiring for the first bramlet Fold was done properly. She had recruited him to check out the electrical distribution grid and had made some adjustments based on his keen inspection skills. She said he had volunteered retire to Mataia and to run the electrical system.

Bram thanked her for her hard work.

Then he asked Lacy for her update.

Lacy commented that her work had almost become invisible to his adversaries, but her team had every one of them tied up in civil or criminal cases and having to use their resources to focus on themselves versus generously giving money to the troublemakers.

She commented that the bubble observation and protection function around the compound area was now being handled by a team that General Tilson had set up.

She shared that she had gotten her father to participate in identifying potential local small extreme antigovernment organizations and had been able to neutralize several of them.

Bram thanked her for her work and for tying up the finances of those funding the attacks.

He asked Marcus if he had anything to share.

Marcus nodded but suggested that they should meet during the week and get into the nitty gritty of what he had been doing. He said that he did not want to bore the entire group with double speak that he would most likely use and though it would be English it would be meaningless to them.

Bram nodded and said that indeed every time the two of them engaged in a meaningful, full conversation about negative Fold space they both walked away dazed. When they ventured to take actual negative Folds, they both ended up lost and needing rescue.

Pat suggested they enjoy a new underwater video that Amy had made on Mataia. It turned out that there were no creatures on land, but Amy had found a variety of underwater plants. She pointed out that Mataia was at a stage where life was just beginning.

Bram enjoyed the video and relaxed. Pat had set his mind at ease with how to manage the oversight committee and the team had provided him with assurance that he had the means to maneuver the oversight committee into a supportive role.

<u>Chapter 13: Waterworld Migration</u>

Monday morning when Bram got to the office, Linda let him know that her sister was in the office waiting for him and wanted a moment alone with him.

He asked Thomas and Bob to give him five before entering.

They both swept the office for bugs and then stepped out.

Bram walked in and asked Lacy what was up.

She said that she had left out a small detail during Sunday breakfast and she wanted to let him know what that was.

She said that she had taken out the three drones meant to hit the barge he was on. She took them out and eliminated the people at the drone launch area.

The truck she blew up must have been loaded with explosives because it sent up a mushroom cloud.

When the jets were coming in, she recalled her attack bubbles that she was personally controlling.

She said that this was the first time that anyone else knew of her actions. She had not wanted to share this during breakfast because she did not want to affect the recognition Matt had received for his actions.

She confirmed that his flying grenades hit exactly where they should have and had she not been there just seconds ahead of him, his attack would have been effective, and he deserved recognition for his actions.

Bram thanked her for waiting to share the information and commended her on her offense. He reaffirmed her decision to keep quiet. He said that he was pleased with her actions and would make sure she received recognition for the excellent work she was doing. He said that she should continue being super aggressive.

Lacy smiled and said that she would and that she had the best job and boss that she could possibly wish for and all the recognition she needed, he had just provided.

Linda called in that the ten minutes were over and almost simultaneously Bob and Thomas entered and said hello and sat down at their seats.

Lacy wished them a good day as she walked out.

Bram looked at the two and asked if they wanted a cup of tea.

Linda announced Marcus's arrival and Bram poured a cup of black coffee and put it across from him where Marcus could reach it.

Fold Wormhole

It was clear to Bram that the weekend outings with his two kids had put Marcus into a positive emotional state and that was his old confident self.

Bram asked what he had learned about the Fibonacci sequence and the way negative Fold space worked.

Marcus shared that the first Fold in negative space did indeed follow the Fibonacci sequence as the bubble Folded out to the initial distance that the bubble had been programed to go. Then the movement at that time period was based on rhombicosidodecahedron points that were generated. The farther out in time that a bubble was programed to go, the larger the rhombicosidodecahedron and the number of nodes that the bubble needed to visit as it tried to return to its launch point.

So far, the only way he had been able to recover a bubble was to program in a routine for it to find the light that broadcast the message "Follow the light" sent out in old fashioned morse code using the laser light magnetron.

He had three bubbles that he figured would someday show up when they finally made it back along the nodes of the rhombicosidodecahedron. He was not sure what century that might be.

He had learned how to set the distance so that the time incremented in one-thousand-year increments. He was now trying to refine the process of being able to select any increment from a year to a billion years. He said that the big accomplishment had been to get a bubble to come back on schedule.

Bram complimented him on his accomplishment and asked when he thought people could safely travel in negative Fold space.

Marcus commented that to safely send people out they would have the same challenge in both the negative Fold space and the positive Fold space. That challenge was to make sure the Fold coordinates were clear of debris. He said that they needed a safety crew certifying that a given coordinate was free of debris. He likened it to Melisa's effort to secure an apartment or house where a bubble could Fold. Once a coordinate was cleared, he felt that Folds to that coordinate would be safe.

Bram said that Marcus had just identified a major barrier to rapid deployment of exploratory teams.

Marcus nodded and said that there would probably be more Bramlet One's as the exploration of space expanded.

Bram said that he wanted to strategically clear the coordinates associated with the needs of their small team.

Fold Wormhole

He then suggested that the rooms that were being used by Melisa for the vacation Folds be emptied of any obstacles that might accidently be moved. He wanted the rooms to be cleared so there was no chance of an accident. It should happen before any more mini-vacation Folds took place.

Marcus agreed to contact Melisa and arrange for that to happen.

Bram said that Marcus should continue doing what he was doing and to enroll Daryl and Harold in verifying that the strategic locations were clear of debris. He asked Marcus to create a list of strategic locations for them to review by the end of the week.

His next meeting was with Mallica and Gerry who were engaged in enabling the Swoshian move to a new water world.

Mallica reiterated the fact that the u-tube design for the Swoshians transport bubbles had greatly accelerated the transfer process. The new vessels had a thirty per cent greater capacity and they were being produced at the rate of three a month at the same cost as one bubble. She had convinced Erica to order as many as could be produced in six months. She was not sure how many they would actually need but figured that the more the better.

Gerry commented that the Swoshians were aggressively moving their population and quickly seeding their new water world with the food supply that they would need. They were synchronizing the speed of their transition with the food supply of the new water world.

He said that it was "aquaforming" versus terraforming and commented that the Swoshian equivalent of environmental scientists were working feverishly to stay ahead of the push to transfer Swoshians.

He had worked closely with the environmental scientists that were helping Amy prepare Mataia to be self-sufficient using them to verify the concept of how to accelerate terra forming if speed were a key factor. He then extrapolated their answers to the Swooshian experience.

Both he and Mallica had reminded the Swooshian leadership that they had a considerable number of years to make the transition to their new water world.

Bram said that it seemed that the two of them had everything in good shape. He asked how many Fold vessels were in use and how was the power to keep them active being generated.

Gerry shared that each Fold vessel had a huge battery that was recharged after each Fold by the light from the sun in each of the two systems. This eliminated the need for large power generation and allowed each vessel to make continuous scheduled trips.

Fold Wormhole

He said that Remi had adapted many of his scout bubbles and other Fold vessels with the same battery design. This had freed up the Dallas power source for the long distant Folds.

Bram said that he was going to enjoy his meeting with Remi. They had been discussing what it would take to reach some of the more distant Fold targets that they had in mind. The amount of energy required had been one of the limiting factors. He figured that now with rechargeable batteries and with the additional available power they would be able to make some of those trips.

Linda buzzed in and let him know it was his ten-minute warning so he could make lunch.

Bram suggested that they all go and meet Pat for lunch and afterwards they would go on with their workday.

Chef D'Carluca greeted Bram and asked if there was anything special that he wanted for lunch.

Bram shook his head and said he was open to anything that he had in mind.

The Chef D'Carluca smiled and said that he had just finished trying a new pork barbeque rib recipe that was smothered with a special sauce. He was anxious to get someone to try it and let him know if it was as good as he thought it was.

Bram said he was looking forward to it and asked if there was enough for everyone.

Pat pointed to the rib on her plate and said that she thought one rib was enough for a meal. She took a bite and said they all should try one because it was delicious.

Bram sat down and told the Chef D'Carluca to bring the ribs on.

Remi came in just as the ribs were being served to Bram and asked if there was enough for him. He thanked the Chef for making plenty and sat down and dug in.

Bram asked if the two could meet after lunch and review what Remi was up to with the bubbles and the new U-tube Fold vehicle design.

Remi had a lot to share, including the fact that he had done little in the way of managing the lab and had turned over the lab back to Lori. He had been focused on the Fold spacecraft improvements.

He had also set up the lab at Einstein City and had tested all the equipment.

The last few weeks had cleared the way for the progress he felt that he had made.

He had Folded all the vehicles of the new design to Mataia so they would not be discoverable when the oversight committee toured the facility.

Bram spent a few moments at the end of lunch and encouraged Mallica and Gerry to set up a celebration meeting with the Swooshians. He wanted to celebrate the ability of the Swooshians to manage the move of their population without the help of anyone from Earth.

Fold Wormhole

He had been worried that support for helping the Swooshians would be a topic that would hurt the current US administration. He now could put that on the back burner of his worry about list.

He knew that the news of the existence of another intelligent species would be a political nightmare, and he decided to avoid all nightmares.

His meeting with Remi included Pat and Amy. Amy and Remi had continued to make considerable progress in getting Mataia able to sustain the initial population of Einstein City.

Bram had coached Pat and Amy on what Earth species to transfer to Mataia. He had made the point that they should strive to introduce the planet to life in such a fashion that they maintained an environmental balance. There was significant guess work in what plant and animal species they should introduce.

Amy shared that she had recruited Thomas's family who were farmers in Iowa. Thomas had shared that his family had decided to sell their farm because they could not compete with the big combines that had taken over the farmland around them.

Thomas said his family was eager to try farming on Mataia.

Amy had not told them about it being on another planet, but she had taken Thomas's father to Mataia, and they had scouted out the farmland on which he said he could supply Einstein City with all the corn, wheat, vegetables, chickens, turkeys, lamb, and beef. He said that he could also supply the milk and butter.

She had promised to provide him the funds to set up his farming operation.

She looked at Bram and asked if they had the money to do what she had promised.

Bram smiled and said she had the go ahead from him but should make sure it fit with the terra forming plans they were making.

He suggested that she engage Thomas and have him educated his parents and the rest of the family that would be making the transition about the fact they would be farming on a new planet.

Amy commented that she thought Thomas's dad would not be surprised because he had looked up at the sun and quoted, "we are not in Kansas are we?"

Bram said that he hoped all of the family cleared security and had no qualms about leaving Earth. He pointed out that with Fold capability they could all still go to family gatherings or take Fold vacations around the Earth.

Bram knew that it was going to take discipline and control to limit the rate of growth of the Mataia population. He felt comfortable in making sure that he and the Fold community, maintained control of their new home.

They would need to establish their own Mataian Constitution that would guide the social order.

He felt he was up to date on all the projects that were underway, and he felt ready to engage with the oversight community.

Fold Wormhole

He was ending the day with a meeting with Erica and Jeffrey to discuss how to bring the oversite committee on board.

Just before the meeting Zoe shared the fact that the leader of the committee had voiced anti LGBT rhetoric during his last political election, but the fact was that he was married in name only and did not live with the woman who was on record as his wife but instead had an apartment that he shared with a man that had been with him for more than twenty years.

She said that he was most likely gay.

Bram thanked her for the information and said that he would make sure that fact either got the leader removed or was used to get him to be a supporter of the Fold effort.

Bram waited until Erica had come into his office and then he placed a video call to Jeffrey.

Jeffrey answered and commented that the meeting was timely because Senator Stately of Utah was insisting on going for a tour of the Fold facility.

Bram suggested that they engage the oversight committee over the next month and that they begin with a weekend outing to the location of the committee member's choice. It could be to anywhere in the world that a Fold facility had been established.

He said that he could send Jeffrey the list of over two hundred-Fold weekend vacation spots.

He asked that Jeffrey have each member select a weekend date and a location to spend the weekend.

The idea was he and Pat to spend the weekend touring with the oversight committee member and at the end of the weekend that member would get a detailed tour of the Fold site in Dallas and be greeted by the Fold community at an evening dinner at the Fold community lodge.

Jeffrey commented that it sounded as if Bram was planning to bribe all the members and pull them into the work of the Fold community.

Bram repeated the adage that honey caught more flies than vinegar. He admitted that he had initially thought of providing the committee with sour vinegar to drink, but Pat had intervened.

Jeffrey said he was glad that it was coming out as a reward to be on the oversight committee. He said that he was putting in his request to take his family to the Kruger National Park in South Africa and go see the elephants, rhinos, and other wildlife. He added that it was one of the items on the family bucket list.

Bram said that his request would be fulfilled. He asked if Jeffrey needed either he or Pat to go along.

Jeffery replied that all he needed was to talk with Melisa, get the Fold location, and make arrangements for the safari.

He then asked Jeffrey to get the desired locations for the rest of the committee members so that those weekends could be scheduled.

Fold Wormhole

Once all the Fold vacations had been taken and the initial tour of the Fold site had been done, Bram wanted to have the entire committee spend a week at the Fold site and get a handle on what was going on.

Jeffrey asked if the script was well oiled, and everyone knew their role.

Bram replied that his team had the best actors a director would want to direct in a fiction movie, and they were all eager to show their stuff.

Jeffrey said he was eager to see the play that Bram was directing and would give him feedback on how good or bad it might be.

Erica had been unusually quiet, but she commented that even he would be surprised at how detailed the play was and how long it would take for the committee to review all the progress reports. She said that her role was to feed the committee every report they might ask for and that she too was magical in her ability to paint a rainbow story.

Jeffrey smiled and commented that he planned to read a good book and let the rest of the committee review all the records that they would be given to review.

He asked that the science advisor, Charles Ford be presented with as much of the scientific information that could be shared. Charles was a great guy that was eager to keep the breakthroughs going.

Bram replied that he was looking forward to meeting Charles.

When the call ended, Bram asked Zoe to check Charles out and give him a report on his inclinations and scientific accomplishments.

Chapter 14: The Committee

A few days later Bram received the list of weekend locations that had been requested.

Senator Stately had requested three seats. He was planning to take his wife and his aid. He had requested a visit to Bangkok and asked that a tour be set up.

Senator Olivia Newton from Maine wanted to enjoy a weekend in Athens with her husband and two children who were still living at home.

Senator Bascom of West Virginia chose to do a weekend in Barcelona with his wife. He wanted to see the Basílica de la Sagrada Família designed by Antoni Gaudi, walk the length of Las Ramblas that stretched from a convent to the port and see the Gothic Quarter and visit the Cathedral of the Holy Cross and Saint Eulalia.

Bram concluded that the Senator had opened a tourist folder and listed it on the request.

And the Science advisor, Charles Ford wanted to go to Lima, Peru. He expressed his interest in touring the trendy bohemian district, Barranco, so he could take in its relaxed vibes.

He also wanted to visit its many museums, see the colonial mansions and the vast ocean views. He asked to have a culinary tour of the restaurants that had international reputations.

Pat commented that the weekend outings would allow her to see places that she had not visited and were very diverse. She said that the detail that Senator Bascom and the science advisor had requested fit very well with what she thought she would enjoy.

Bram agreed they would have interesting weekend outings. He said that he did not plan to do any business on the trips. He wanted to spend time in making sure that everyone had an enjoyable time. He planned to focus on getting to understand the committee member.

He engaged Melisa and asked her to develop a full and very interesting tour at each location. He suggested using private tour guides that would provide a solid and educational tour.

He asked Linda to set up the Monday afternoon luncheons at the recreation center and have her family cater the event. The attendees should include everyone that was engaged in one of the projects. He suggested that she strategically seat each committee member with the Fold team players around them that was well versed on what the committee member was interested in.

Linda asked if it would be better to avoid having the multiple Monday afternoon luncheons and have only one where all the Oversight Committee members were present.

They would then be able to exchange stories of their trips and bond with each other.

Bram thanked her for the suggestion and agreed they should have the luncheon when the entire committee would visit the site. He wondered about adding a Fishing outing at their favorite park.

Linda said that her family would be able to cater that event and suggested that the luncheon and fishing trip be merged. She commented that she would arrange to have the fishing boats. She laughed and said that the bullet holes in the boats had been repaired and they all looked brand new. She asked if the boats should come armed.

Bram said she should check with Lacy to see if there was any apparent threat on the horizon.

Bram then asked that she make all the detailed arrangements for the weekend mini vacations with the committee members.

Linda checked with each of the committee members to determine where they were to be picked up.

The pickup point for Senator Stately was to be Washington DC. Melisa gave Linda the address of the Apartment building on 24th Street NW where she had a long-term lease on the entire seventh floor corner of the building. She had just recently tested the coordinates and had cleared one room that was the bubble receive-transmit room.

The pickup point for Senator Newton and her family was to be in a house only a two-block walk from the Governor's house on Green Street.

She told Linda that she was not sure where the senator lived but she figured the Senator would know where the Governor's house was located.

Linda learned that Senator Bascom wanted to also be picked up in Washington.

Science advisor, Charles Ford and his wife wanted to be picked up in Boston. Melisa let Linda know that she had secured the entire fourth floor of an apartment building on Prince Street.

Linda thanked her for the information and said that the information would be sent to each of the committee members.

She then contacted each of the committee members and agreed on the pickup time and date and asked about what they would like to see during their weekend vacation tour.

Once she had the dates for each of the committee members she arranged for Bram and Pat to arrive the morning of the day before. She worked with Pat to arrange the Friday tour and the dinner location.

Linda felt she had set a record in getting all committee travel arranged and also arranging Bram and Pat's outings.

She called Melisa and thanked her for making it possible to get everything done. Melisa said that after going to seventy-six different countries she had exhausted her personal desire to travel and was ready to just go fishing.

Linda sympathized with her and said she felt much the same way after getting everything arranged.

Fold Wormhole

She let Melisa know that Bram was planning to host another fishing outing with all the committee members present.

Melisa gave a laugh and said that she had a new Kevlar jacket that she was going to wear on the event. She commented that Bram had yet to have a fishing event that didn't include a dramatic gun battle.

Linda agreed and said that her parents were catering the event and had commented about the same thing. They had approached Lacy about making sure she had her defense technology in place. Lacy said that it was not hers to command, but she was sure she could talk the General to be "at the ready."

Lacy commented that the Fold community had the top-level offense going and it was currently in action against all their detractors.

Her parents had let her know they would all be taking their weapons with them.

Bram was pleased with Linda's update and the fact that he and Pat would begin the cycle on the coming Friday. He thanked Linda for setting up the Friday tour to several of the out of the way places in the DC area that Pat had requested.

One major location was the National Arboretum to see the Corinthian columns that had been in the inaugural background of Andrew Jackson and Abraham Lincoln inaugurations in 1829 and 1861 as they stood outside of the Capitol building.

At that time, the columns were still part of the Capital building. Now they were sitting by themselves in a stark, open field supporting nothing but air. The primary attraction of that site for him was that it looked down on the most stunning cherry blossoms display along the Tidal Basin during spring.

Pat had also requested a visit to the International Spy Museum to take in the tools of espionage. She commented that it claimed to have the largest collection of spy-related artifacts in the world.

The third request was to go to the National Bonsai Museum where she wanted to see a Bonsai tree that dated back to 1625 and had survived the Hiroshima bombing.

Linda said that she had arranged for a professional tour guide to take them on their tour and to show any other unique places that she had knowledge of if it fit the visit time frame.

She had left the choice of the lunch location up to the tour guide, but Linda specified she wanted it to be upscale. The dinner was to be at one of the top restaurants in Washington and was going to cost Bram one of his better nickels.

Linda let Bram know that she, Pat, and Zoe had spent time going over the menu of top restaurants at all the pickup and destination sites and had decided on which ones to try.

She then shared the evening meal menu for Washington DC.

Fold Wormhole

Bram commented that he was looking forward to the Washington tour and the very interesting dinners. He asked that she set up an informal introduction call with Senator Stately and to let the Senator know that his request was being fulfilled and give him the pickup address.

He suggested that Linda contact everyone else and let them know that their request would be fulfilled.

He asked if Pat and Zoe had already set up their before tours at all the pickup locations.

Linda said they were going to spend Thursday morning setting up the next three trips.

Bram nodded and said that was perfect and he said he knew he was in for a treat.

The next morning, he was ready to visually meet the Senator. He had asked Zoe and Eric to stay outside of the office so he would not have to explain the protection situation.

Linda placed the call, which was answered by the Senator's support. The two of them conversed and soon Bram was connected with the Senator.

The Senator took the lead, introduced himself, and voiced his interest in the Fold project and his concern about the finances.

Bram chose to ignore the bait and followed his script of greeting the Senator and making the offer to demonstrate the Fold capability by taking the Senator, his long-time partner and his wife to Bangkok and then completing the on boarding process at the Fold compound on Monday.

Bram had specifically made it a point of mentioning the long-term partner. He wanted to bring the Senator out of the closet. He was not going to let the Senator remain in the political closet that he was hiding in. He was not going to share top secret information with someone that was not confident enough to be open about his personal life.

The Senator changed his challenging tone. He must have sensed Bram's direct nature because he then focused on the Fold to Bangkok and asked if there were any issues with the request.

Bram replied that it was quiet acceptable, and two rooms had been secured at one of the top hotels at the center of the city. A top tourist guide would take them to the requested locations and would arrange the tour so that they would have lunch at one of the top restaurants.

The tour would end at the hotel early enough for all of them to refresh themselves and then they would be escorted to another world-class restaurant.

Bram let the Senator know that his support had been briefed about the restaurants and the meal selections.

He said that the arrangements at the Fold facility on Monday would go into all the details he was interested in.

He asked the Senator if he liked to fish.

The Senator replied that he had been an avid fisherman before getting elected and taking his seat in the Senate. He said that fishing sounded great.

Bram smiled and said that his fishing trips always resulted in everyone landing their share of fish. He did not mention that everyone also participated in a gunfight.

He let the Senator know that the entire Oversight committee was being scheduled in for an entire week and at the end there would be a celebration fishing picnic.

Bram reminded the Senator that the address for his Fold pickup had been given to this support and ended his end of the conversation by saying he was sure the Senator would find the weekend and his Monday visit to the Fold compound enlightening and that he would leave as a staunch supporter of the breakthroughs that would make the US the global leader that it was meant to be.

He asked the Senator if there were any questions about the upcoming visit.

It was clear that the Senator was on his heals, as he shook his head and said he would be at the pickup address at the appointed time.

After the call, Bram asked Linda to come into his office. Zoe and Eric accompanied her in and the four of them reviewed the interaction with the Senator. Linda shared her interaction with the Senator's support.

Zoe asked how Bram planned to introduce the FBI bodyguards.

Bram commented that they would all Fold together and tour together. He shared that he and Pat planned to Fold to DC on Friday and then they would all Fold to Bangkok as a group.

He asked Zoe to find out if the Senator's wife lived in Washington.

Zoe replied that she already had the background check feedback on the senator and knew that his wife lived back in Utah. She commented that she figured that her participation on such short notice was at best a fifty-fifty proposition.

He looked at Zoe and let her know that he knew that she was part of planning the Friday tour and dining and she should not pretend that she was unsure how he was planning to introduce her and Eric to the Senator. He commented that he had never kept her in the closet.

Zoe asked why he had asked to have the two of them wait outside during the discussion with the Senator.

Bram smiled and said that he was betting that the Senator was going to be surprised by what he was going to find out and that he wanted to overwhelm the Senator and convert him to being a Fold supporter.

He was using the FBI security as of the one surprises.

He was going to use Bramlet One and the lab environment as a second surprise.

He would use Wheel One and Amy as another surprise.

He was going to use the Fruit Farm production as a surprise.

Fold Wormhole

He was going to use the fishing experience as another and final experience. During the picnic, the General would introduce the protection system and Lacy would introduce the Fold offense.

He figured the Senator, and the entire oversite team would leave as a supporters or the Fold Team would be leaving to Mataia.

He brought out the fact that the Senator faced an upcoming election. He was going to ask Lacy to help the Senator make it through the next election if he became a supporter of the Fold effort but if the Senator still insisted on trying to control the Fold project, he would ask Lacy to begin a negative ad campaign against the senator.

He made the point that the Fold project was too important to have a committee focused on obstruction.

Zoe smiled and said that she would never tweak his nose again.

Bram smiled and agreed that he was exposing one of his mean streaks.

The early Friday morning Fold was the first Fold using the new inverted U tube design. Remi escorted them out to the tube and spent a few moments getting everyone oriented. He pointed out that tube with six rows of two seats was the biggest model that had currently been produced.

He commented that the project would have versions all the way down to two rows of two.

Remi pointed out that every seat had the same controls but would only have control of the bubble if they engaged their computer and only one computer would be allowed to be in control.

Bram got in and commented on the comfortable seat and the spacious area around the seat.

Remi said he figured it was time to upgrade the Fold experience. He pointed out that the craft was powered by a rechargeable battery that converted sunlight into electricity. It could still be charged by plugging into an outlet but now it could travel anywhere in the universe and not run out of power.

Bram congratulated Remi on the improvements and then said he was ready to go to tour Washington.

On arrival, Bram looked around the receiving-departure room and noted that his request to clear everything out had been executed.

He stood by as Zoe and Eric cleared the apartment. He took a moment and asked Pat how she had come up with the unusual tour stopping points.

Pat chuckled and said that Zoe and Eric had both suggested what to see that would be different.

After they all took their suitcases to their rooms they took a quick tour of the apartment and Zoe commented that Melisa continued to get great apartments and appoint them exquisitely. She was glad that Bram had such a good budget.

Fold Wormhole

Bram informed her that his budget had not put up a single penny and the Melisa had set up the weekend vacation program and any longer vacation as a money-making venture. She had set up the Fold Travel Agency LLC and had set up the books so she could legally manage the associated cash flow. He figured she would be one of the most affluent individuals in the Fold community.

He then followed Pat out of the building.

Pat was greeted by the tour guide that was a young woman that ran her own private tour company. The two and Zoe had met online and were chatting like old friends.

Bram liked the technology that connected people so quickly. He followed Pat into the Van. Zoe and Eric sat behind Stacy the guide. He noted that the driver was a youngish looking Black man that was introduced as Dikembe.

Stacey listed the order of the tour and said that she was pleased to do a tour that allowed her to go to a different venues than she normally toured.

At each location Bram took in sites and learned about stuff that he had not ever thought about but that filled in pieces of history that was interesting to him.

The columns removed from the white house and now standing out in a field made him wonder what else could become a tourist attraction.

The Spy museum was more interesting, and he enjoyed learning about a field that he had never pursued.

The length and the details of the tour proved to be about right.

Then they went to lunch and enjoyed a meal that rivaled the best they had recently eaten. The walk around the neighborhood that followed allowed Bram time to think about his meeting with the Senator.

The tour continued and the evening meal once again was of great delight.

Starters.
    Jumbo Lump Crab Cake
    Calamari Fritto Misto
    A Clam Platter
    Arugula & Fennel Salad
Main.
    Surf n Turf, a Petite Filet and Lobster Tail
    8 oz Center-Cut Filet topped with Crab & Shrimp sauce,
    Lobster Béarnaise, Classic Oscar
Sides.
    Wild Mushrooms, Fresh Asparagus, Broccoli Parmigiano, Tuscan White Beans,
    Creamed Spinach, Shrimp Risotto
Desert.
    Strawberry Delicacy; strawberry panna cotta, makrut lime gelato, honeycomb brittle

Bram commented that he was glad to share and glad that Zoe had an empty leg to fill because just the starters were enough to fill him.

Stacey and Dikembe were both at the meal and they said that they had never eaten at the restaurant because of the cost, and they had never eaten so well.

Pat said that she was going to have a bite of everything and share anything she had ordered but her desert would be all hers.

Bram decided on following Pat's "a bite of everything" and at the end asked her for a bite of her desert.

Fold Wormhole

At the end, as he leisurely sipped on a hot tea, he realized that he was definitely ready for a long walk.

Chapter 15: The Senator

Bram was up early. He went down to the kitchen to make pour over coffee. He was not surprised to find Zoe there ahead of him doing the pour over. Eric had set the table and had a variety of jam set out. He was standing at the toaster buttering the toast as it popped up.

Bram had grown to think of the Zoe as his younger sister and Eric as his brother-in-law. It was hard to think of them as fierce fighters who had repeatedly demonstrated the reason, they had been chosen to be his bodyguards.

Zoe was a petite woman that was lithe and athletic but somehow seemed too frail to have repeatedly demonstrated a world class athletic talent.

Eric was more rugged, but he too did not seem the type that would run toward gunmen who were shooting at him, but Bram had watched him do so.

Bram took a seat at the table and put some strawberry jam on one of the buttered toast. Zoe brought over a cup of coffee and asked how the night had been.

Bram joked about the fact that the pea under the mattress had kept him up most of the night.

Pat had come to the kitchen and commented that his snoring is what had kept her up all night.

Zoe joked that her hollow leg had emptied, and that hunger had awakened her early and she was ready to do it all again.

Bram asked Eric what his complaint might be.

Eric commented that his bed partner had kicked him all night as her leg emptied, and he was hoping that the bruises would not prevent him from wearing his shorts over the weekend.

Bram enjoyed their banter and fake complaints.

He was satisfied with three pieces of toast and was ready to make the transit to Bangkok.

He went to his room, packed his suitcase, and rolled it out into the living room.

They all sat down and wondered who would be standing on the other side of the door when the time came to make the Fold.

The Fold would occur roughly fifteen minutes later than the given schedule. Bram had arranged it so he would have a moment to greet the Senator and whoever was with him and then introduce Zoe and Eric.

The doorbell jangled right on time.

Bram walked to the door and opened it.

Senator Stately and his partner were standing at the door. Bram took note that there was no wife.

Fold Wormhole

He brought the two into the living room and introduced everyone.

The Senator introduced his partner as David Conden, a lifelong friend.

He then asked about Alex and Eric.

Zoe stood up and replied that she and Eric were Bram's permanent bodyguards and were required to be on duty twenty-four seven. She explained that there were two more FBI bodyguards back at the compound and that they rotated their daily assignments.

The Senator commented that he had been unaware that the FBI had assigned bodyguards to Bram.

Eric gave him a brief description of the dozens of times that Bram had been attacked. He said that there was also a contingent of Marine guards that accompanied them whenever they were outdoors.

The Senator asked what the risk was of an attack on the weekend.

Bram replied that it was very low, but they would be cautious.

He then said it was time to load up and led the way to the room where the Fold tube would materialize.

He opened the door to an empty room.

He had the Senator stand outside the room and watch as the Fold unit materialized.

After a moment of silence, the Senator asked how such a thing was possible.

Bram commented that it was a matter of luck and advise from Einstein and led the way to the back of the unit and put his weekend bag into the bin located to the right of the entrance. He then stepped in and walked to his seat at the front. Pat followed and walked up the other aisle.

The Zoe had the Senator enter and go up the aisle toward Bram and David go in and up the aisle toward Pat.

Eric entered next and followed David.

Zoe entered put her things in the bin and closed it, closed the entrance door, and took her seat behind the Senator.

Bram gave a brief explanation of what they should expect. He asked that everyone put on their seat belts.

He then sat down and pressed the fold button.

Almost instantaneously they were in a similar room and Bram announced they were ready to disembark.

The Senator commented that he hadn't felt a thing.

Zoe opened the bin and the exit door. She and Eric got out and said that everyone should relax for a moment until they had cleared the apartment.

Moments later she announced that it was all clear and that they should disembark and see what a dramatically beautiful apartment Melisa had provided. She said she had no idea where they were in Thailand, but the view was stunning.

Fold Wormhole

The apartment was the entire fifth floor that had four bedrooms a very large living room and a very well-equipped kitchen and an enclosed veranda. The air conditioning provided a very clean and refreshing environment.

Pat commented that Melisa had told her that the apartment looked out on the Chao Phraya river over to the Wat Arun Ratchawararam Ratchawaramahawihan area that had an ancient Buddhist temple, with an iconic, ornately tiled central spire as its main attraction.

Everyone agreed that the view from the top floor was stunning.

Bram took the Senator to one of the bedrooms and suggested that he and his partner consider enjoying the room. They could call and cancel the two rooms at the hotel. He pointed out that it would give them a much better chance of all of them getting better acquainted.

The Senator hesitated for a moment and seemed about to turn down the offer.

David nudged him and quietly said, "John, they know," let's take the room.

Bram knew that he had just witnessed a breakthrough moment.

The Senator nodded and said the room would be great.

Pat said that their guide was out in the van waiting for them. She reminded them that they had left the US at eight in the morning and that in Bangkok it was eight in the evening, and their tour would be to go to one of the upscale restaurants where they would all enjoy a local dinner.

Then for the next two days they would hit the spots the Senator had requested, and a few additional ones suggested by the guide.

They followed the young woman guide into the restaurant. A waiter led them to a private room that had a large round table with a Lazy Susan. They were all equally spaced around the table. The lazy Susan featured a wide assortment of Thai dishes and various sauces. The waiter pointed to each dish and gave the Thai name, and the guide gave the name in English. There was a bowl of Spicy Shrimp Soup, a bowl with Spicy Green Papaya Salad, a steel pan with Thai Stir-Fried Rice Noodles, another one with Fried Rice, another with Fried Basil and Pork and different version of noodles referred to as Guay Teow that meant Noodle Stir Fry. Then there was a bowl of chicken with Cashew Nuts, another with Green Chicken Curry, a platter of Thai Spring Rolls, a platter with Holy Basil Stir-Fry with Pork, a bowl of Mango and Sticky Rice, stir fried beef, a half of pineapple filled with fried rice, and an additional salad with strips of beef.

Once the waiter had described all the food, he asked if there was some additional dishes they might be interested in.

Bram laughed and said that if they ate half of what was on the table they would set a record for how much they could eat.

The waiter then took their drink orders. There was a choice of wine, beer, or nonalcoholic drinks. The group settled for a bottle of red Syrah and a bottle of Chenin Blanc.

The Lazy Susan seemed to be in constant motion as each person randomly selected a dish to try. If a particular dish ran low it was replaced with a full serving.

Pat commented that it was hard to keep track of how much she had eaten and whether she had tried every dish.

Zoe said that her approach was to try each dish in the order that it was on the Lazy Susan. Then she gave a groan as one of the waitresses rearranged the dishes as she brought out a new dish.

The Senator commented that he had given up hope and was just eating whatever stopped in front of him.

Their guide informed them that they could take anything they wanted back to their apartment.

Bram asked her if she would like any of the dishes and found out that she and her driver would love to have any of the dishes that were left on the table, and they did not want.

Pat told her to ask to have the remaining dishes put into carry out containers and that once they were in the van, all the dishes would be available to her.

She suggested they order several bottles of wine to take back to their apartment and an assortment of nuts and other small snacks.

Each of them carried out a bag with the leftovers and put them in the back of the van. No one was interested in taking any up to their apartment.

Pat thanked the tour guide and driver for having taken them out and verified that they would go out for a morning breakfast and then go on tour.

They all returned to the apartment and after getting the snacks served on trays and pouring the wine, they sat around talking about the great food they had just tasted.

Zoe asked David what he did while the Senator was in the senate and learned that he did research to help the Senator understand the issues associated with various bills and proposals. Later in the evening the two of them would discuss how the bill would impact their state or how they would trade their vote for support on bills important to their state.

Bram found that interesting and asked how often bargaining for support or for granting support took place.

The Senator commented that it was going on every moment of everyday and sometimes it was difficult to determine what was going on.

Fold Wormhole

In the morning, the guide let them know that she was taking them to her cousins small restaurant. She said that they could eat anything for breakfast that they wanted but she had asked her cousin to make a small amount of several dishes. She said that one dish was a thick rice porridge known as Joke. Soft boiled eggs in a shot glass that was one of her favorites would also be available. Another dish was just rice and an egg omelet. A sausage, egg, and cheese biscuit would also be available. The Thai version of a donut made with a slightly sweet dough and deep fried with a fluffy inside and a crunchy outside would also be on the table. Sticky rice topped with custard and wrapped in a banana leaf, fried bananas, coconut gridle cakes would all be available to try.

And a wide variety of cut fruit such as mango, guava, papaya, pineapple, watermelon, rose-apple would be featured as well.

She said that they could have as much to eat as they desired and did not have to try everything. She said that lunch would be taken at the Floating Gardens and Dinner would be at a restaurant that her parents owned.

She asked if the arrangement was satisfactory and that if there were any objections she would make the desired changes.

Zoe spoke up and said that she liked the fact that they were connecting the tour with her relatives restaurants.

The Tour on Saturday was to the Greenville beach for an early morning walk or a casual seat with the view of the sea then they would drive across the city to the Taling Chan Floating Market where they would have lunch. During the drive to the floating market, they would pass a number of tourist spots that she would highlight and stop if there was interest to do so.

Pat said that sounded like a good plan.

The floating market had a wide variety of shopping that was pointed out by the guide. She had rented a boat that was taking them all along the various shops.

Bram was soon bored with the shopping portion, but he took in the lifestyles of the vendors in the various boats. He was personally not enthralled with the sights and was soon thinking about the Fold exploration he and Marcus had discussed.

He was relieved when lunch time arrived, and they got out of the boat and went into a sit-down restaurant. He was not really hungry and settled for a mixed salad and a soft drink. The local soft drink was on the sweet side and had a flavor that he thought was what mango and lime juice would taste like.

He was ready for the ride back to the apartment and a long hot shower before going out to the guide's family restaurant.

He was more interested in how the family restaurant would be managed and its hygiene. He had been negatively impressed with the noon time restaurant.

Fold Wormhole

The Senator commented that the Floating Market was interesting but did not capture his interest. He said that so far the morning walk along the beach was the highlight of the day.

David seconded the opinion and said that the floating market had been his idea, but the beach was a much more enjoyable experience.

Zoe said that the fish that she had for lunch was great and was the highlight of the visit to the Floating Market.

The guide began to apologize but Bram stopped her and said that she should not take it personally. She was doing a great job and was fulfilling what had been requested. He said that he was looking forward to the evening dinner.

Once back in the apartment, Bram voiced the fact that he was a little overwhelmed with all the eating and not enough exercise. He took a shower and then spent the early part of the evening doing floor exercises.

Pat sensed that Bram was bored. She knew he was focused on influencing the Senator and turning him into a Fold program supporter, but it was something that Bram had no patience for.

She was going to see if she could move that process forward.

Bram was sitting in the living room relaxing while waiting to go out to dinner. He was pleased to have the Senator join him.

Bram engaged him and shared the fact that the Senator should be able to use his role as the leader of the oversight committee to expand the number of supporters that would vote for him.

The Senator agreed that it should help. He reminded Bram that he was running in a state that was extremely conservative and that deficit government spending was of great concern.

Bram pointed out that the Senator could position his role as strengthening the power of the US. He pointed out that the Senator could not directly divulge the details of the Fold capability, but he could insinuate that it would make the US the most powerful nation on Earth.

He then suggested that he should also take the opportunity to leverage his role to come out of the closet.

The Senator asked if Bram was joking.

Bram said he was not. He said that he would never support someone on the oversite committee who was willing to hide the love a person had for another just to satisfy a group of biased uninformed individuals.

He said that he would help the Senator win his next election if he was willing to come out of the closet. And he was prepared to make sure the Senator lost the election if he did not.

He made the point he could not share the details that made the Fold process work with someone who was not honest.

The Senator said that he was shocked at what Bram had just shared. He asked what made Bram think he could keep him from winning re-election.

Bram pointed out that the Senator had just told him how conservative his supporters were. How would they react if the lead up campaign adds highlighted the faggot in the closet.

Fold Wormhole

The Senator commented that he had never met a person that was so direct and so clear.

He asked what the alternate ads would be.

Bram commented that it would show the Senator standing with the Senate building and the Statue of liberty in the background and him saying that Utah was the staunch supporter of the US being a world power.

He asked who Bram knew that would help him get re-elected.

Bram called Zoe in and asked her who the financial supporters of the Senator were. Zoe pulled out her phone and read off a dozen names and the amount each had donated to the Senator's re-election fund.

Bram asked her what would happen if the Senator went public with the fact that he was gay.

Zoe said that most donors would base their support on how the Senator could wield the power of leading the Fold oversight committee. She was certain that the Senator would win even though it might be by a tight margin. She commented that she had enough information on each of the donors to be able to influence their public response and to help them open their pocketbooks.

The Senator shook his head. He commented that he had never faced such a choice and would wait to respond after they were back at the Fold compound.

Bram said that would be appropriate and timely.

The remaining tour of Bangkok went smoothly and the tour of the temple directly across the river was a highlight.

They had scheduled the Fold back to Dallas to take place in the morning since that would be Sunday evening there and it would give them the evening to relax and prepare for busy Monday morning of touring the Fold site.

Bram had instructed Linda to give the Senator the vanilla tour, meaning that no detailed information would be shared. He was waiting for the Senator to share his decision of whether he was coming out of the closet.

The Senator commented that he had not expected the amount of work and progress that the organization had made.

Bram joked that it had all been made possible with little money being spent.

He commented that so far the Fold project had spent less than six hundred thousand dollars.

The Senator said that he was expecting a much larger number and was looking forward to seeing the books.

Bram wondered how the Senator would react if he learned about the Swooshians and the help that had been given that allowed them to move from one planet to another. That was information that Bram was going to withhold for as long as he thought necessary.

Fold Wormhole

He knew that the technology would change the world economy and that learning about the Swooshians would shatter the belief that humans were the only sentient beings in the universe.

When they moved from one side of the Fold compound to the other, the Senator commented that it seemed that a small army was protecting Bram.

General Tilton was in the van with them and replied that going fishing with Bram had proved to be like going into battle. He shared the stories of past fishing expeditions and the role that Bram had played in each.

The Senator replied that the stories seemed a little exaggerated.

It was clear to Bram that the General was a little bit miffed with the Senator's attitude.

The senator was Folded back to the starting location when the evening came to a close.

220

Chapter 16: The Rest of the Committee

The team Folded into a home that was right on Willard's Beach where they were to meet Senator Olivia Newton and her family. This was a different location than the one that had originally been selected because it provided a better Friday experience.

Pat, Bob, and Thomas had talked through what to see in the Portland, Maine area and had decided on a sailing cruise in the afternoon and then an evening seafood meal at a top restaurant with a harbor view. The three of them had agreed that taking it easy was the way to take in a Friday night after a busy week.

They were all meeting for dinner at one of the top seafood restaurants and then they would return to Willard's beach and Fold to Athens which would put them there at roughly three in the morning.

They figured that they could get a quick nap in and then take a morning walk on the beach.

In Athens, the Fold was into a top floor apartment across from Kalamaki Beach.

When Pat commented that the apartment had enough space for all of them and suggested that they all stay in the same apartment. The senator welcomed the offer. She agreed that it would give them all more time to get to know each other and to enjoy the beach.

She made the comment that Senator Stately had ranted about the exorbitant expenditures that the Fold project had made and had convinced the committee that money was being wasted but after experiencing the Fold from Maine to Greece, she said it did not matter if the Fold project had spent billions of dollars. The technology would place the US in the lead in almost every technological field she could think of.

Bram smiled and said that he had spent a great deal of money, but he had not yet made it to a billion. He made the point that the most money spent to date had been to set up the Fold vacation spots around the globe and it was being managed as an investment with a three year pay back and no money had been from the Fold budget. The Fold to a location was free but the cost of the living quarters were part of the cost of the vacation package.

The Senator asked what she owed for her vacation.

Bram smiled and said that this first one was on him, but any future ones would be charged.

Fold Wormhole

Pat sensed the ease with which they were all getting along and knew that Bram now had two for sure supporters on the committee, Senator Newton, and Jeffrey. She put Senator Stately in the maybe list.

The tour of Athens and the Greek ruins went as planned and the food was as good as always.

After the weekend and her tour of the Fold compound, Senator Newton was a little overwhelmed with the exploration already done by the Fold team and the ability of the team to produce its own equipment at such a low cost.

Just before leaving, the Senator again thanked the Fold team and pledged to support the efforts that were underway.

Senator Bascom of West Virginia chose to do a weekend in Barcelona with his wife.

Senator Bascom left West Virginia as a sceptic but after spending the weekend in Barcelona and enjoying the tour and dinners, he came around and was more supportive but voiced his one remaining concern about the open nature that decisions were made. He felt that it should be more structured and managed by the leaders.

Pat had hit it off with his wife and the two had spent their time walking together and talking. It was clear to Bram that Pat had had an inside track on influencing the Senator. He figured that the Senator would most likely come around to being a full supporter but at the moment he was on the maybe list.

The Science advisor, Charles Ford chose to go to Lima, Peru. He and his wife were very pleasant to be with and it was clear he was eager to understand how the Fold process was even possible. He kept asking if it was real.

Without exception every member asked it if the bodyguards were necessary. Pat explained that from the very beginning Bram had faced repeated attempts on his life. She shared that the attacks now numbered more than a dozen. She said that back at the Fold compound the number of bodyguards doubled in number because there was the FBI and the Marines both providing guards.

Bram, Pat, and their bodyguards made all the trips except the one with Jeffrey. He and Pat decided to surprise Jeffrey.

They Folded to Maputo, Mozambique to the eleventh-floor apartment that was the Fold location. They had dinner with he and his family before they were scheduled to Fold home.

Maputo was the closest Fold location to Kruger National Park and the location where they could all go out to dinner.

Pat asked Melisa to recommend a restaurant that seemed to offer one of the better menus.

Jeffrey was surprised by the impromptu dinner notice, but he and his family commented that it was nice to be engaged with friends.

Jeffery was also impressed with the fact that it seemed that Bram had turned the oversight committee to one that seemed like it was going to be supportive.

Fold Wormhole

Linda had kept track of all the travel and had managed the scheduling of work that Bram was doing with Mallica, Marcus and Remi. She was surprised at the stamina that Bram displayed and the ease with which he managed the transition between the travel and then working with the various teams.

The week that the entire oversite committee was meeting at the Fold compound was a busy one. Linda had set up the main auditorium as the central meeting location for the committee and had scheduled a series of presentations and then mini tours that followed each presentation. She had designed the week so that it was a constant flow of information and then the showing of what the information had just described.

General Tilson gave the physical tour of the Fold Facility and explained how it was protected and that over time they had raised the level of protection to the point that it was as secure as the Fort Knox facility.

Melisa gave a tour of the housing area. She highlighted the recreation center, the ball fields, and the homes. Several people gave spontaneous testimonials about what a great place the Fold community was to raise their kids.

Erica took them through the Green House production area that was now in full production of the U-tube design Fold vehicles. The only Fold vehicle present was the one that had been used to transport the committee members in.

Remi gave them a tour of the new Lab facility and highlighted the research he was doing and had several test machines running just for show. He wasn't really running any experiments, but it appeared that his team was doing their research.

Marcus shared how he verified that a point in space was free of debris so that what happened to Bramlet Number one would not happen again. Bramlet One was the center piece and Marcus asked what had caught the attention of each of the Senators when they had Folded in and out of the Arrival-Departure rooms. He pointed to Bramlet One and said that the rooms were totally empty to ensure that those coming and going did not end up like poor Bramlet One.

Amy and Pat highlighted Wheel One that along with the destroyed Wheel Two had been the first vessels to take people out to the other side of the moon. They commented that the rapid progress that had been made had made both wheels obsolete and they added that the two of them had gone from being Fold pilots to unemployed.

Bram commented that how Fold affected the human body was a field of research that was now full time and would be on going for the near future.

Senator Newton asked if it had a negative effect on the body.

Fold Wormhole

Pat responded that she had done extensive testing, and the Fold process seemed to fix the defects in the body. She commented that the Fold process had eliminated scars and burn marks on various members of the Fold team.

Committee Science Advisor Ford asked if it reduced hay fever symptoms. Pat smiled and said that she thought so, but she only had her personal experience to base that on and had not run any scientific research in that area. Ford said he thought it might because his normal hay fever seemed to have disappeared.

Mallica spoke up and commented that the Fold process would open opportunities that had yet to be recognized but it would certainly have a dramatic economic, social, environmental, and medical impact.

The Oversight Committee should plan on managing how each of those areas would be handled. They should also be considering the pace at which any of these opportunities were rolled out. If the timing was not well controlled global chaos would be the outcome.

Senator Stately nodded and commented that never in his dreams had he thought that the Fold technology would be as powerful as he now thought it would be. He commented that his initial approach had been petty and if Bram wanted to spend more money he was in full support.

Jeffrey spoke up and commented that the Fold effort had spent less than five hundred million dollars. He pointed to Bram and commented that they were looking at a penny pincher that was leveraging every dollar he had in his budget.

The most money that Bram had spent was on the housing for the personnel working on the Fold process and on building the facility that they had all now toured.

He laughed and joked that the extravagant spending was to take the committee fishing and have a picnic.

Linda stood up and commented that it was time to end the day's meetings and go and enjoy a fine dinner at the pool side facility.

She reminded everyone that the departure in the morning would be at five in the morning and that there would be a breakfast box for each person. The vans would take everyone to the boat pier where they would get assigned to one of the ten fishing boats that had been arranged to take them out.

Bram led the committee out of the auditorium and suggested they all walk to the poolside recreation facility.

Had anyone been looking it appeared that a small army was making its way on foot.

Fold Wormhole

Suddenly Orlando started a chant.

Took the bite, took the fight
Took it from the Oversight.
Nasty people's exoneration
Now in support of our great Nation.
One, two, three, four.
Took the bite, took the fight.
Took it from the Oversight.
Oversight, Oversight
Just a bit short of being right.

Soon they were all jogging, singing the jingle and laughing

Later Bram thanked Orlando for having come up with the ditty and said he had missed him and his ability to lighten the day.

The mood of the evening dinner had been raised significantly by the jog over. The committee members all commented that they had not expected such a warm welcome and they really liked the ditty that they had joined in singing.

Elizabeth nodded and said that in her lifetime she had never worked with a person who seemed to enrich and empower people the way that Bram did.

At various times during the dinner, a committee member would stop and thank Bram for having arranged the mini-weekend vacation that had been used to get them to understand the marvel of the Fold process.

He thanked them and commented that there was an unimaginable future for the technology and that they would all need to be very careful how the capability was communicated and deployed.

The dinner ended early, and Linda reminded everyone to get a good night of sleep. She said that if they were not use to Bram time, waking at five in the morning would be sleep shattering for almost everyone.

The next morning everyone managed to get to the vans on time and the hot cups of coffee were greatly appreciated.

Bram was personally wide awake and ready to go fishing. He now saw the oversight committee as a group that was going to be supportive. He was also hoping that the fireworks that Linda had planned would be the only fireworks of the day.

Ted met them at the park and led them all down to the pier. Linda assigned people to the boats and soon they were leaving the pier and gliding through the dark on a placid smooth lake.

The millions of stars overhead seemed to have twins shining back from the depths of the dark lake water. The only sound was the smooth purr of the boat motors that seemed to have embraced the night and were happily pushing their boat smoothly through the water.

Bram had his arm around Pat who seemed to be dosing. He looked over at Senator Stately and saw that David was leaning against him also dozing. The Senator nodded and gave Bram a thumbs up.

Fold Wormhole

The sun was threatening to break over the far mountains when Tom cut his engine and let the boat glide forward on its own momentum. The other boats fanned out and stopped as well.

Bram noted that if he were looking from above the boats would look like a flock of geese in a V formation floating on the surface.

Tom shouted for everyone to wake up and throw their lines in.

Bram watched as the Senator took the back fishing chair and pointed for David to take the bow seat.

The boat was a little crowded. Zoe, Eric Pat, Tom, and he had to find a place from which to fish. The two spots on either side of the motor were perfect for Zoe and Pat.

He and Eric each fished off the sides in the middle of the boat. Tom had a small pole that he was using from the boat's driver seat.

Senator Newton and her husband were fishing out the sides of the boat and her husband and her two children were sitting in the main fishing chairs.

The fishing was as bountiful as Tom had promised and by the time the sun had hit its zenith, everyone had at least one nice catch.

Bram had put away his pole immediately after catching a nice bass. He then enjoyed watching everyone else as they talked to each other and displayed a fish they had pulled in.

He complimented Tom for taking them to a spot where everyone seemed to be lucky.

Tom chuckled and said that the fish could not resist the bait he had spit on.

Pat moaned and said she was now, for sure, going to give him her catch.

The Senator had just pulled in a huge fish and commented that he wanted a bottle of the spit.

Tom said that he would think about how much he would need to charge to make it worth his while.

He then called out that it was time to head back to the park for the picnic lunch.

Once they were back to the park, Linda informed Bram that the fireworks she had promised was going to take on a very different look than she had been imagining.

Linda said that when she had discussed this with Lacy, she had been reminded that the picnic was during the afternoon and regular fireworks were just not going to be very effective. She said that Lacy was going to put on a surprise demonstration with the fleet of protective bubbles.

Bram replied that he could hardly wait.

Not long after General Tilson introduced Lacy. He made an announcement that they were going to demonstrate how versatile and beautiful their fleet of protection bubbles could be. He asked everyone to look out to the center of the lake.

Fold Wormhole

Clear bubbles with flashing lights that cycled between green, yellow, and red burst one at a time from the surface of the lake and rose rapidly into the air. As they rose the bubbles formed into V formation and fired tracer bullets that left a blue trail behind them. The bubbles swept into the sky, made a dive toward the park, and then rose and went straight into the air. They then made a long loop and disappeared into the water. Suddenly one at a time they shot up at the end of the pier and shot up into the sky.

They were so well synchronized that there appeared to be three parallel yellow, green, and red streaks rising into the air. As they reached their peak, a huge explosion sent out a rainbow-colored mushroom cloud. And suddenly all that could be seen was the trail of the rainbow colors slowly falling back to the surface of the lake. And then there was nothing!

Senator Newton's two kids, Marcus's two kids and Jeffrey's two led the cheering that rose up from everyone in the Park.

General Tilson was speaking on his phone letting the people that had programed and had controlled the attack bubbles know that they had outdone themselves. He held up his phone so those controlling the bubbles could hear the shouting and cheering.

Charles, the science advisor walked over to Lacy and complimented her on the choreography and synchronized dancing of the bubbles. He said he was amazed at the Fold versatility and flexibility. He said that he was ready to join them and learn how he could use his skills in the Fold program.

Senator Stately complemented the Fold community on their ability to embrace, entertain and envision the Oversight Committee. He said that he was returning to Washington a changed person who was going to work to ensure that the Fold program had a green light going forward.

Bram saw the sunlight being broken by something coming fast across the lake. He walked over to a marine who was holding a scoped rifle and asked to borrow it.

As soon as he saw what had caught his eye he ran toward the dock and began firing.

He could hear Lacy shouting for everyone to get down and the general shouting on his phone to get the attack drones online.

Bram kept firing hoping the lead he was putting in front of the incoming drone would have an effect.

Suddenly a huge explosion hurled him back and he lay on the ground hoping no one was hurt.

He rolled over to look to where the food table was still standing, and Marial was straightening it out.

He was shocked.

Lacy shouted that there were three more incoming drones but suddenly a swarm of attack bubbles appeared and quickly took them out and then flew on toward the far shore like a swarm of mad hornets.

Bram sat up as explosions across the lake sent small mushroom clouds into the air. Then a huge explosion sent a much larger one up.

Fold Wormhole

The General was talking into his phone and asking why it had taken so long for the protective response and wanted to know who was asleep.

Bram stood up and handed the rifle back to the Marine who he had taken it from and thanked him. The Marine nodded and said he had more ammo anytime he needed to use his weapon.

Bram went over to the kids and asked if they were all right. They all gave him a hug and said they had a ditty.

> *Took the fight, Took the fight.*
> *Showed it to the Oversite.*
> *Shoot, Shoot*
> *Rat-tat-tat, Rat-tat-tat*
> *Blew it,. Blew it, out of the air.*
> *Took the fight, Took the fight.*
> *Showed it to the Oversite.*

Senator Stately looked at Bram and commented that he now believed everything that Bram had shared and that he planned to accept the challenge of coming out of the closet.

Bram asked who the committee had shared their schedule with and learned that all had shared it with their personal support staff.

The Senator gave a laugh and said that other than being blown on his butt the fishing and picnic was the most exciting thing he had done in his life, and he was now ready to eat.

He pointed at the General and said that he had gotten an earful of Marine language as the General tore someone a new one for being asleep at the switch.

The departure of the committee members at the end of the day was to be from the park. Ted's three catering vans had been positioned to form a U that would shield the Fold vessel from sight.

After a picnic that every committee member swore was the most exciting one, they had ever been invited to and featured the best food they had ever eaten, they got into the bubble and were returned to the Fold hangar where each got into a different bubble and were Folded home.

Bram sat down at the picnic table and pushed Zoe into having the FBI trace the leak that had occurred.

Zoe commented that she had already launched the search, and she would let him know as soon as she learned where the leak led.

A few days later Zoe reported that one of Senator Stately's aids had obtained his schedule and had shared it with his office members.

One of the office members had sent the schedule to an opposition candidate in Utah that was planning to run against Senator Stately.

That candidate had shared the schedule with some of his supporters. It turned out that one of the supporters was a member of a far-right group that decided to eliminate the Fold leadership.

They had access to some older drones that could carry a significant amount of C4 and had decided to attack the picnic and eliminate the committee and as many Fold personnel as possible.

Fold Wormhole

The first drone had almost succeeded. It was the one that Bram had shot down.

Bram shared this finding with Senator Stately and said that the Senator now had the ammunition to take out his political opposition.

The Senator replied by sending Bram the political advertisement that announced his run for re-election and clarified that he and his partner of more than twenty years were looking forward to keeping Utah well represented and being the leader of the group that would have oversight responsibility for one of the top scientific projects that would put the US in the technical and military lead globally.

He also included a blurb by his wife that also endorsed him as the right person for Utah as the right man, at the right time and in the right position. She constantly repeated, "Utah Senator Stately loves thee! And will make you great."

Bram was pleased with how the tone of the committee was now one of support versus one of control and adversity.

The detail of the leak highlighted how easy it was for the opposition to learn about what was going on in the Fold project and made him much more sensitive on what information should be shared.

He was pleased with the fact that the information about the water worlds, the new world and the negative Fold learning was still under wraps. He was going to reinforce keeping it all a secret for the foreseeable future.

Jeffrey and his wife let Bram know that they not only had a great weekend vacation and had enjoyed the surprise dinner with he and Pat, but they were now feeling that the role at NASA would be much easier than they had anticipated.

Bram smiled and said that it appeared that everyone was to have an easier time than they had expected.

Chapter 17: Election

Bram was not usually very attentive to the political scene. However, this midterm election was different.

Senator Stately had come out of the closet.

Bram had promised his support. He made sure that Lacy connected with all his financial supporters and made the case why they should make certain that the Senator won and remained the leader of the Fold oversight committee.

Jeffrey and his wife campaigned in Utah for the senator. It turned out that Jeffrey's wife was the one that was having the most positive effect. She had gotten together with the Senator's wife and together they had attended multiple rally's where they spoke of his upright character traits, honesty, and the power he yielded in the Senate.

The other factor was the three times daily political add that featured the Senator and commented that he was the right person, in the right role, at the right time and the smart people of Utah would be crazy to lose the influence, control and the financial benefits that the Senator gave the State of Utah.

Each ad began with "Land of the Pioneers, Utah Senator Stately loves thee!" and ended with the state motto of Stately supporting "Industry." One was the state tagline and the second was the state motto.

The senator won a resounding victory. He called Bram and thanked him for the help he had received for his campaign and said he was still trying to figure out why the Fruit Farm located in Dallas had run the overwhelmingly successful add campaign that his staff said had been one of the major reasons for his resounding victory.

Bram replied that he had promised the Senator a win and having the Fruit Farm do the ads was his way of delivering that promise.

The Senator thanked him and simply said David had commented that they both owed Bram one.

Senator Bascom of West Virginia seemed on a sure path to a humiliating loss. He had opposed the bill that would have provided a much-needed support for his poorer supporters, and he had voted for a bill that opposed abortions. A much more liberal candidate had a ten-point margin going into the election and came out the victor.

Senator Newton of Maine called Linda and left Bram a message saying that she was going to encourage the Massachusetts Senator to volunteer for the opening on the oversight committee.

Fold Wormhole

She said that the Senator, though from the other party was the type of person that would complement the committee. She suggested that if Bram was in agreement, Linda should find out where in the world the Senator would like to go for a weekend vacation. She was personally sure that she had the ability to get the support to seat the Massachusetts Senator.

Bram was pleased to have been given the heads up by Senator Newton.

The election turned out to be a good one for the President who was able to keep control of both the Senate and the House. It was also an election that allowed John Stately to assume the life that he had shunned because of politics.

Zoe looked into the Massachusetts Senator's background and found out that the Senator was a black woman whose grandparents had been brought over from Gabon. It turned out that her grandparents had been sold to the slave traders by a clan that was the enemy of the tribe her grandparents were part of. They had been told they would go to Brazil and be slaves there, but a storm took their ship off course, and they ended up coming to Virginia where they were auctioned off to a cotton farmer in Georgia.

Zoe found out that the Orungu clans at Cape Lopez organized a kingdom whose power rested on control of the slave trade through the harbor at the mouth of the Ogooué River.

The Mpongwe clans of the estuary, who were already important traders, also profited from the slave trade, as did the Vili people of Loango, whose activities extended throughout southern Gabon.

She learned that only the Fang, who were migrating southward from Cameroon into the forests north of the Ogooué, refused to hold slaves or engage in warfare to obtain them.

She said that she had not realized that black people were selling other black people into slavery.

Zoe said that she had talked to the Senator who let her know that after the Civil War her grandparents had moved north and ended up in Massachusetts. They had chosen that state because at the end of the American Revolution, Massachusetts had more free black people than slaves, and by 1783, Massachusetts had abolished slavery. They had been aware that Boston was a destination point for the Underground railroad and had heard about Boston's tightly knit Black community that provided a place where they were welcome.

Later they had moved out to Worcester where they both had been able to find employment. Her parents had grown up there and had later moved back closer to Boston where they worked in one of the large hotels for most of their lives.

Fold Wormhole

Zoe commented that she had looked up the Senator's name and found out that her first name Bonank meant, "finds wealth at home," and it seemed that the Senator acted that way. She was very tight with her family and publicly always highlighted what a great family she had.

Her parents had been born and raised free and they made sure she went to college. She had struggled at first but after two years in a junior college she had been able to make it into Boston University and had focused on getting a law degree.

Pat commented that it seemed that the Main Senator was reaching across the aisle to select another woman and a woman of color. She said that her respect for Main Senator Newton had gone up significantly.

Bram asked Linda to contact the Massachusetts Senator Etaing and learn where she would like to spend a weekend vacation.

He was not surprised to learn that Gabon was where the Senator wanted to visit.

He asked Melisa if she had a Fold location in Gabon and was pleased that there was one.

Melisa commented that Gabon was seen as the friendliest country in Africa. She had found a place in Libreville, the countries capital. The apartment was on the fifth floor of a building that was along the sea and had several restaurants within walking distance.

She said that she had a tour guide that had taken her to several locations and highlighted the Gabon historic past.

Zoe commented that the Senator had mentioned she wanted to visit the city of Ndjole that had been the place where her great grandparents had been born and raised during their early years.

Melisa looked that up and said that it was probably a couple hours' drive and then a few hours at the city and then the drive back. She said she would call the travel guide and get the details.

Bram asked her to verify the Fold delivery-departure point.

Melisa let him know that the delivery-departure point would be a few blocks from the waterfront below Bunker Hill where she had rented the entire seventh floor of a building. It had a great view of the USS Constitution, and several other ships anchored in the harbor.

Two days later Linda let Bram know that Senator Etaing had asked if her parents could be included on the trip to Gabon.

Bram replied that as long as they could get a secret clearance and signed a non-disclosure agreement it was OK with him.

Zoe let him know later in the day that Senator Etaing's father had an arrest record. He had been part of the marchers on the Edmund Pettus Bridge and had been arrested and convicted of being part of a riot.

Fold Wormhole

Bram shook his head and asked if the FBI could clear up that situation and get the record expunged. He was convinced that the politicians in Alabama needed to get hot irons put under their rears so they would clear up the kind of mess they had created in the past.

A few days later he got a call from Senator Etaing who thanked him for having helped to clear her father's name. She said that she was impressed with his influence because she had been trying for years to do the same thing. She said that her mother wanted to have dinner with he and Pat when they got to Boston.

Bram said that he looked forward to it and would really enjoy eating at a restaurant that catered to the black community.

Later in the day Senator Etaing called him again and said that her mother had decided to host the dinner at her house because her friend that had a restaurant had closed it. The Senator wanted to know if that would be acceptable.

Bram said that it was, but he reminded the Senator that four FBI bodyguards would follow him while in Boston and two bodyguards when in Gabon and asked if her mother was ready to feed a small army.

The Senator laughed and said that dinners at her mother's house was always like eating with a small army. She said that she was sure that her younger sister and her husband and her younger brother and his wife and their two kids would all be there.

She suggested that Bram prepare himself for a house full of loud, laughing, crying, and singing people.

After the call Bram asked Zoe to check out all the family members. He commented that it all seemed normal, but he wanted to make sure.

Bram called Jeffrey and asked about Senator Etaing and whether he was in support of having her on the Oversight Committee.

Jeffrey replied that he was very enthusiastic as well as supportive. He added that the committee would be much more well-rounded, balanced, and enjoyable.

Bram then asked Linda to offer Senator Bascom condolences on his loss and to remind him of the sensitive nature of the information that he had acquired about the Fold program.

He was concerned that the Senator would try to use what he knew about Fold to try and raise a campaign war chest. He asked Zoe if she had any friends who might be willing to keep tabs on the Senator's actions and give them a heads up if there were any indications of improper information sharing.

Zoe replied that she had a woman friend that had family in West Virginia and based on her dislike of the Senator's stand on women she would love to keep tabs on him.

That evening, Bram had Zoe update the rest of the team on the upcoming Fold activity of getting Senator Etaing on board the Fold Oversight committee.

Fold Wormhole

He then asked Pat to suggest what they should do during the day in Boston before going to dinner at the Etaing residence.

Pat suggested they get a walking tour guide but limit their walk to going to the USS Constitution Museum and then walking up to the Bunker Hill Monument and then having the tour guide take them to the Etaing residence.

Bram asked how everyone felt about that limited tour itinerary. Everyone agreed that it would fit into a Fold on Friday afternoon, give them a slice of history, and keep them focused on the dinner.

That next day Bram consulted with Marcus and asked him how the negative Fold calibration work was progressing.

Marcus commented that he had been able to get the calibration of the time by learning how each increment of distance affected time in the negative Fold realm. He had learned that for short increments linearity could be assumed but as the distance factor increased the linearity went out the door and he then could not figure out the relationship.

He suggested that Bram get involved so that they could figure out the relationship of time and distance and be able to control time.

He admitted that he had made multiple attempts at postulating a theory and then spent time trying to prove it, but all his theories were failures, and he was stumped.

He had asked for Mallica's help and she had proposed some interesting ideas, but they had not panned out. They together had again been stumped.

The two of them had gotten online with Zuri and the three of them had tried additional ideas but they all agreed that they needed help.

Bram agreed to focus on determining how to control time in negative Fold once he was back from his next Fold with the new Oversight Committee member.

The Fold to Boston was flawless and they arrived on time to go out and meet the tour guide who took them first to the USS Constitution Museum where she took them slowly through the museum and related the history of the USS Constitution and emphasized the fact that it was still a battleship that was on active duty.

They then drove back to the other side of the turnpike and then began the walk up toward the Bunker Hill Monument. On the walk up they passed several older buildings that the guide pointed out had been present during the Bunker Hill battle. She added that several of the owners had participated in the battle.

They reached the monument and got its history. She explained that the battle was actually misnamed because the majority of the action took place on Breed's Hill and that is where they were standing.

Fold Wormhole

She pointed around the perimeter of the park and said that about one thousand colonial militiamen under Colonel William Prescott built earthen fortifications on top of Breed's Hill because it was closer to Boston.

She shared that it was during this battle that the Colonel knowing his men were short on ammunition is said to have shouted the words, which became famous, "Don't fire until you see the whites of their eyes!" She shared the fact that this was often disputed but seemed to have survived as where that saying had originated.

She went on to explain that Patriot gunfire cut down some 1,000 British troops, with more than two hundred killed and more than 800 wounded. More than one hundred Americans perished, and more than 300 others were wounded. She pointed out that because of sheer numbers the British defeated the Americans.

She underlined the fact that the Americans that survived, escaped, and avoided being captured by the British because Peter Salem, a Black soldier, shot and mortally wounded Major John Pitcairn, the British commanding officer who was leading the final charge up the hill.

She highlighted the fact that Benjamin Pierce a father of the future U.S. President Franklin Pierce had fought in the battle.

She then explained that the first monument was a wooden pillar dedicated in 1794 to the memory of the most famous hero of the battle, Joseph Warren and was funded by the King Solomon's Lodge of Freemasons.

The larger battlefield was left largely undeveloped and unmarked until 1823, when an elite set of New Englanders that included Daniel Webster and Edward Everett, who were incorporated as the Bunker Hill Monument Association set out to build the current monument.

In 1825 one hundred thousand people gathered on Bunker Hill to watch the famous Frenchman, Lafayette lay the cornerstone and listen to a speech by Daniel Webster.

But fund-raising went slow, and construction lagged and by 1828, though most of the granite had been quarried, the funds to continue raising the monument were lacking.

The guide related that the Bunker Hill Monument was conceived as a way to express the gratitude of the American people for the sacrifices of the American soldiers who fought at the battle.

In 1830, believing that the lack of attention to the monument indicated a weakening of American patriotism, Sarah Josepha Hale began a campaign in her Ladies Magazine to raise funds from American women to complete the monument. In 1840, Sarah Hale organized a Ladies' Fair in Boston, where a number of women's organizations raised the final $30,000 to complete the work.

The monument was dedicated on June 17, 1843.

The guide made the point that it had taken almost fifty years before the current obelisk replaced the old wooden monument.

Fold Wormhole

Bram commented that he had learned more about the battle for Boston than he could have imagined. He pointed out that they had used their afternoon well and that Pat had identified the perfect way to spend their time.

Pat thanked Bram for his kind words and pointed out that it was time to go to dinner at Senator Etaing's parents' home.

She led the way back down to the van.

As they arrived at the address of Senator Etaing's parent's home Bram made a comment about all the cars parked on the street and in their yard. He wondered just how many relatives and friends were going to be present.

The Senator came out to greet them.

Bram noted that she was more petite and slenderer than he had anticipated.

Zoe, Eric, Bob, and Thomas all got out first and fanned out among the cars and made sure all was clear before Zoe gave him the "all clear sign."

Bram then exited and held his hand for Pat to grab as she got out.

The Senator came over and gave Pat a hug and then turned to Bram and hesitated a moment until she was sure he was willing to get hugged.

Bram smiled and bent slightly so that the two could hug. He liked her already because he was a hugger.

The Senator asked them to call her Bonank or Bon and not Senator.

Bram introduced his FBI bodyguards.

The Senator greeted them and commented that he was one of the first persons she had interacted with, other than perhaps the President, who traveled with four bodyguards. She asked who he had offended to warrant such protection.

Bram nodded and shared the fact that he had been attacked about a dozen more times than the President and the four persons that she had just been introduced to had saved him every time. She was looking at decorated warriors of the highest degree.

The Senator said that they were going to get attacked by her family, but they were all friendly and meant no harm.

The Senator then led the way in and soon Bram was overwhelmed with smiling greeters welcoming all of them letting them know that they were going to enjoy the best dinner they had ever eaten.

The younger kids soon had Zoe and Eric down on their knees playing marbles with them.

The Senator's father led them to the living room where they could sit and talk.

He watched as Bob and Thomas scouted around the room and then assumed positions at each end.

The Senator's father commented that he wished he would have had their kind of protection when he had gone on the freedom marches. He said he still carried the scars that he and earned.

Fold Wormhole

He thanked Bram for clearing his name and for agreeing to include he and his wife to the weekend mini vacation that Bonank had said they would take. He also said that he and his wife had signed the non-disclosure agreements and were both surprised that they had received secret clearances.

He asked how that had all been arranged when Bonank had been trying for years just to get his name cleared of the charge of being a criminal.

Bram smiled and replied that the wheels of justice sometimes just needed to be kicked in the butt and knowing where to kick was a specialty of one of his FBI bodyguards.

The Senator came in and sat down. She bent her head and said that her mother had pressed her to ask if her brother and sister might be able to be added to the trip.

Bram smiled and replied he was not sure and that he would check. He called Zoe over and asked her if such a request could be fulfilled.

Zoe asked Bram to step outside for a moment. As they went out to the front yard, Bob, Thomas, and Eric spread out among the cars.

Zoe said that she had checked out all the family members and they were all hard-working lawyers or doctors. If Bram agreed, she could get temporary clearances for the Senator's brother and sister. She said that she doubted that their spouses or children could go.

Bram nodded and said that they should get the temporary clearances and have the brother and sister sign them before boarding the Fold transfer vessel.

Zoe led the way back into the house and into the living room.

Bram noted that Pat was engaged in a conversation with the Senator's father and mother.

The senator looked up and beamed a large smile when Bram nodded his head up and down.

She then commented that she was hopelessly compromised as a member of the Oversite Committee, but she did not care. He had changed the lives of her family, and she owed him a lot.

Dinner featured three styles of barbeque chicken, a mac and cheese that had small chunks of ham in it, greens that had a unique vinaigrette dressing and a buttery smooth whipped mashed potato.

Bram tried some of each dish and was soon filled. He pushed his chair back slightly and said that he had eaten so much he had to push back from the table.

The Senator's mother brought in a peach cobbler and some small bowls and a bowl of vanilla ice cream. She dished up a bowl of the cobbler and gave it to Bram. She said she had used fresh peaches to make the cobbler and always left the skin on so that the cobbler got a deeper taste and often a pink hue.

Bram took a bite and commented that he hoped heaven would be as good.

Pat jokingly asked what made him think he would be going to heaven.

Bram replied that he figured she would make sure to put in a recommendation for him that would carry some weight.

The Senator's mother commented that anyone that had helped her family the way that he had would have her prayers and if she got there first she would make sure to put in a good word with St. Peter.

Bram thanked her and then looked around the table. He commented that he had eaten with a group of interesting folks, and he hoped that in the future they would be able to do it again.

He then said that it was time for he and his team to get back to their apartment and get a few hours of rest.

He suggested that those that were making the trip with Bonank get a few hours of rest as well because they would arrive early at their destination and then leave immediately on a long day of touring.

He reminded everyone that departure would be at midnight, and they should all gather at his apartment a few minutes prior to that time.

He then got up and like magic, his four FBI bodyguards got up thanked everyone for their friendliness and thanked Bonank's parents for their hospitality.

Pat gave Bonank's mother a hug and let her know that she would love to get the peach cobbler recipe.

Bram then turned and walked toward the front door following Bob and Thomas. He knew that Eric and Zoe would be bringing up the rear.

Chapter 18: Gabon

The tour to Gabon was somewhat was less exciting than Bram expected. The countryside was interesting but his recent journey through the Scandinavian scenery had seemed more enjoyable. Or maybe he thought he was getting used to having his life on the line while being attacked.

He decided to focus on getting to know the Senator and her family and listened to many of their family stories. He had overheard the Senator tell her mother that she might have to change parties because she was being treated with more respect by the folks in the opposition then she was being treated by her own party.

It reminded Bram that he did not care about a person's party affiliation. He focused on their behavior and what they did and if they acted with integrity.

He was personally opposed to giving special privileges to those with extreme wealth and power, but he also was not willing to personally spend his time trying to defeat a specific person who had other ideas about that situation.

He figured that everyone should pay a fair share of the taxes it took to run the country.

He knew that his position in the Fold organization gave him access to monetary funds that he would not otherwise have but he had made sure that his personal income remained in the middle of the pack for scientists in the US.

The freedom to follow his mind into new areas of development and study was much more important than monetary wealth or power.

The weekend outing had given him time to think more about how time and distance interacted in the negative Fold universe. He wondered if the linkage to the past put the person making that linkage physically able to step into that past. If that were the case the people in the positive Fold environment would be able to travel back in time and physically interact with it.

For all he knew someone in his future may have had already done so. He was the discoverer of the link. He knew that it had been formulated in his mind and it had been done so through a tedious and very puzzling process. But eventually in the future others would gain control of the Fold process and would most likely discover the ability to go back in time and potentially alter it.

He wondered how he could set up a test that would unveil such actions.

Fold Wormhole

He decided to run an experiment to see if his theory of being able to step out in the past was possible. He was personally afraid that it would be possible. It would mean that he had unleashed a power larger than any current weapon possessed by man.

He thought everyone should be very afraid of such a power.

On his return from Gabon, he gave Senator Etaing the tour of the Fold facility and then took her whole family fishing out on the Columbia river. The outing was almost as big as it had been for the entire Oversite committee team several months earlier.

Ted and his crew took them out where everyone caught fish and the shouting back and forth was boisterous and laughter filled.

It was clear to Bram that the Etaing's enjoyed each other, and they treated each other with love and respect.

After returning to the park and while they were enjoying the picnic every member of the family made it a point of stopping at his table and thanking him for the great time that they had experienced

Bram was touched by the Senator's mother when she said that she had never had such a great weekend and that the fishing outing showed her a man that had captured her heart and one who she was going to make sure her daughter remembered when tough decisions about the Fold program came up and had to be made.

The Senator sat down at his table and commented that it was going to be tough to be on the oversight committee because she was so overwhelmed and impressed with the work he was doing. She commented that she was equally impressed with the loyalty and support all his people had for him. She said that it spoke to her of a person who should get all the support he desired.

Bram thanked her and let her know that he was always more impressed with the way people acted and carried out their role based on the principles they held dear. It mattered not if the decisions were what he wanted but it mattered that they were made with fairness to all involved.

The Senator smiled, nodded, and replied that he just kept making her life harder.

Marcus was sitting at Bram's table and quietly commented that he had to put up with Bram and his fair attitude every day and he as well had to live Bram's motto of "treat others as you wish to be treated." He smiled and said that everyone in the organization could state Bram's motto and they all knew that the simple saying had a huge impact on the entire organization.

He ended by saying Bram was an example for them all.

The Senator thanked him for the comment and said that it would become her motto as well.

That afternoon she and her family all went to the airport. The Senator had let Bram know that she was flying back with the rest of the family, but she looked forward to her next opportunity to Fold to some exotic location.

Fold Wormhole

The next day as Bram and Marcus began their meeting, Marcus commented about how much it meant to him to work with him on the Fold effort.

Bram thanked him and then said that they were going to try a simple experiment to see if travel to the past was possible. He said that he had Linda close and lock the viewing room. She had cleaned the white board of all writing and taken a picture of the board. This would serve as a time stamp.

He said that the two of them would enter the negative Fold universe and go back just one day and enter the viewing room using the coordinates of the bare floor that could hold their two-person Fold vehicle.

They would then write a message on the board and date it.

He asked Marcus what that message should be.

Marcus smiled and said that if it worked, instead of "Kilroy was here," they should write "Bram and Marcus were here" put a sticky note on the board that gave the time and date and imprinted by Linda with her notary stamp.

He suggested that they have Linda, Pat, Amy, and the bodyguards all go in first and ask them what they saw on the white board.

He added that if it was possible he might faint.

Bram commented that it would make everyone's life change and secrecy a thousand more times important.

They both walked to Linda's desk and asked her to witness the writing of the message and to put her notary stamp on it.

Linda asked if what was happening was connected with having locked the Viewing Room.

Bram smiled and said that her intuition and smarts was why he had selected her to support him. He asked her to call Pat and Amy and have them come to her desk. He then told her that the three of them and Zoe and Eric would open the viewing room and be the witnesses of what was on the white board.

Linda waved the note and said that if this ended up on that board she would most likely faint.

Bram nodded and said he might join her as well. Then led the way to where the Fold vehicles were located.

Bram asked Marcus to put the room's coordinates into the negative Fold program. He turned on the negative Fold return beacon that had become the key to being in the negative Fold realm. He then asked Marcus to initiate the Fold.

Marcus let out his breath and pointed to the blank white board that was next to the Fold vehicle. They both got out and Bram asked Marcus to put up their message.

Marcus wrote "Bram and Marcus were here" and stuck Linda's note at the end.

Bram decided to add a personal note. He wrote, "Take a deep breath, don't faint but our world had just changed dramatically."

He then said that it was time to follow the light and see how long it would take to return to their current time.

The return was almost instantaneous, and Bram let out the breath which he had held.

Fold Wormhole

Marcus led the way back to Linda's desk.

He stopped at Linda's desk and thanked everyone for being willing to be a witness. He suggested they all take a deep breath and walk slowly to the viewing room.

Zoe did the opposite as she led the way and walked faster than normal to the Viewing Room.

Zoe broke the silence by saying that she had never been more nervous. She went on and stated that being practically nude in a gun battle had been nerve racking, but this situation was mind altering and it was one time where she thought she knew the feeling of fear.

Bram was aware that adrenaline was running high in everyone.

He asked Zoe to unlock it and then lead the way in.

It was clear to Bram, who was feeling anxious, that Marcus was very nervous.

He was very sure that the message would be on the white board.

Zoe fell to her knees in front of the board and reach up and took the notarized note down and read it.

Bram walked up to the seat he normally used and sat down. In spite of knowing, he still felt shaky.

Pat sat down next to him and put her hand on his. She quietly said that his break throughs just kept happening and this particular one was as Zoe had stated, mind altering. This one she was a little more personal in that it meant that the past might be able to be altered.

Bram nodded and squeezed her hand but had nothing to add.

Linda sat down in front of them. Zoe handed her the notarized note and asked if she had really signed and stamped it just twenty-five minutes earlier. Linda nodded and said that it was also recorded in her notary logbook.

Amy sat down on the other side of Bram and put her hand on his. She commented that maybe she should have left him in the desert when she had the chance. She pointed at the board and said that it would take more than a deep breath to ever take that picture of the message out of her mind.

Bram finally found his voice and spoke what was on his mind. He said that this moment was not to be recorded in any physical fashion and no one should share what they had been witness to.

He said that someday in the future things might change but for the foreseeable and maybe their lifetime, it had to be kept a secret. He commented that he had been worried about how the Fold technology would disrupt the world and now he was more than worried, he was somewhat terrified.

Fold Wormhole

Zoe commented that if he was terrified she was petrified. She could not stop thinking about how the world around her could be altered without her knowing.

Bram commented that they might need to do more experiments to learn if they could tell when things had changed around them. He was curious if there was a way to know if a person would sense that change had occurred.

He replied that she was right about how she was thinking and that protecting him had taken on a new meaning. She and her partners were now protecting all of society. Their role had taken on a new greater and challenging scope and responsibility.

He chuckled and suggested they go and relax at a sport that they all knew how to handle and do something dull like fishing.

Eric smiled and said that going fishing with him had just taken on a new meaning as well. It usually resulted in a gun battle but that was small stuff as compared with the future being able to go back in time and join the gun battles.

Marcus had been quiet and finally commented that he had been thinking about how he should coach his kids. He was now not sure how the future would transpire. What guidance do you provide that you were confident would help them.

Bram emphasized his belief that the fundamental principles of truth, honesty, integrity and treating others as one wished to be treated remained the basis on how people should behave and that those fundamentals would be what allowed them all to live with this new capability and they would continue to hold the fabric of society together.

He made the point that his concern was about the fact that a sizable portion of society did not live by those unchanging values and principles and that portion posed a significant threat.

He then asked Amy, Marcus, and Linda if they were willing to be on a team that used the negative Fold realm to investigated the people that he would ask Lacy to name. Their objective was to identify any planned action against the Fold program.

Marcus commented that they were being asked to become time spies.

Bram nodded and said that like all spies they would remain unseen and covert.

The team left the Viewing Room a changed but still solidly aligned one and one that would follow Bram's guidance.

Bram once again made the rounds of all the projects and got caught up on what each had accomplished or any barriers they faced.

He realized that his perspective had changed. The knowledge that history could be altered had him thinking about how the Fold effort might be affected. He planned to be on the offense and keep from having to play defense against the unknown future.

Fold Wormhole

Erica brought forward the first current issue. She shared that their production facility in Seattle was going to close unless they paid a holding fee to keep the space available to them.

Bram said that they should not pay any holding fee. He was not sure if they would ever wish to build the size of Fold transports that they had built for the Swoshians. He said they should take the chance that it would be far enough into the future that if they needed to, they would negotiate a new fee for the use of the facility.

He suggested that Erica work with Pat and Amy to look into determining the cost of building a basic but large enough structure on Mataia and use the money they would have used for extending the contract to make it happen.

Erica nodded and agreed that she would do so and most likely make it happen sooner versus later.

Thomas volunteered to move to Mataia and manage the construction of such a facility. Bob said if Thomas got to go, he wanted to go as well.

Bram thanked Erica and responded to Thomas and Bob that it would all depend on timing and the action taking place at the current Fold facility.

He then suggested they all go to lunch.

They were just minutes late, but their normal table was occupied by Marcus, Mallica, Pat, Amy, and Lacy. They took the next table and then went and got their lunch.

It was clear to Bram that the morning discovery that the negative Fold space could transport them back in time and they could physically interact in that time frame had them all envisioning different scenarios.

He personally knew that eventually he would be using it to protect the Fold program. He was not yet sure how he would do that, but he would do it legally and he would try not to negatively impact history in any major way.

The negative Fold universe was an area that needed careful study, and it needed safeguards that would keep people from making a mess of the flow of time. He would need to work on that safeguard but until he made that breakthrough, he would work hard to keep it a secret that only his team knew about.

Chapter 19: A Fold in Time

Bram had shared his concern about how easy it was to get into negative Fold space. Pat agreed with him that safeguards needed to be put in place. She suggested that the entire work that he had done with negative Fold somehow become invisible. She suggested that he purge all mention of the negative Fold work and that the information about it be put in a place where only he could access.

Bram thought about it and said that he would move everything to do with negative Fold space to Mataia. To work on negative Fold, one would need to be on Mataia and would need to reinitiate the placement of the control module that needed to be in position halfway into negative Fold space to gain access.

He said that he would only train one person to be capable to do such a thing.

Pat suggested Zoe for that role.

Bram asked her why it should be Zoe.

Pat responded that Zoe had become an ardent believer in his philosophy and her protection role would be very complementary to the effort and she would also need someone else's help to do anything in the Negative Fold realm.

He agreed but said that it still left too big of a door into that realm.

Then while working on a presentation, he was working on, he experienced being in a software loop.

A light went on.

He quickly programed a loop for the control of going into the negative Fold universe. He designed it so that if the step back into the negative Fold universe was attempted from Earth, the Fold vehicle would go to a jail-like cell on Mataia and then immediately return to its original coordinates. The person in the Fold vehicle would, in a fraction of a second, be back at the starting point of the Fold. If by chance they happened to figure out how to jam the loop, they would be in a jail cell on Mataia that would signal him in his time of that situation.

He decided to try it with Marcus without telling him about the loop.

After several loops, Marcus got out of the Fold vehicle and said that there was something wrong with the controls.

Bram then let him know about the do loop that he had programed into the control system.

He explained that they could disable the loop when they needed to but otherwise it stayed on twenty-four seven.

Fold Wormhole

Bram made the point that only the two of them would know about the loop. He also highlighted the fact that the loop would be set up so that if someone tried to Fold into negative space, the loop software would count and report on how many times it had been attempted.

Marcus commented that he was now with Zoe about never playing poker against him. He would never trust any game since he now understood that he could be manipulated by someone in the negative Fold space.

Bram nodded and agreed that the knowledge about negative Fold had altered his thinking as well and had him thinking hard how to keep anyone from creating chaos in the flow of time. He said that for him the flow of time from its beginning out to infinity was now no longer as simple as he had once envisioned. He went on to ask the question, "has someone in the far future already reached back and altered the events that we are now experiencing?" He then asked, how long will my attempts to keep humans from going back in time stay in place?

When will some very smart person realize they are in a loop and break through the loop that I have programmed?

Marcus shook his head and agreed that it was only a matter of time before such a thing could happen. He pointed out that the technical changes that the Fold technology represented would significantly increase the technical capability of society and what usually followed was that the scientific side also made significant strides.

That knowledge increase would mean that the person that would break through the loop would not have to be even closed to being a Bram. They would have the aid of new technology.

Mallica and Gerry came to his office and let him know that the Swooshian sun had accelerated its death throes and was expanding more rapidly than the Swooshian scientists had predicted. The evacuation was now happening at the fastest pace that was possible. Every Fold to the new water world was packed beyond its maximum capacity.

Gerry said that the Swooshians would make it off their current water world with time to spare and then they would focus on getting out all the species Folded to their new environment. The new water world would be ninety-nine percent the same as their previous world. It would have one percent new plants from their new water world that the Swooshian were making certain survived.

Mallica shared that Ohaan who she considered a Bram equivalent, had sent thanks from all the Swooshian leaders for the aid that they had received. They sent an invite for Bram to visit so he would see how they had populated the world that he had found for them. They shared that their celebration display would feature one thousand Swooshians rise from the water and jump through the air in a synchronized display.

He suggested that his Earth counterparts partake of their celebration drinks and food and watch the most extensive Swooshian display ever put on.

Fold Wormhole

Bram asked what the Swooshian's ate.

Mallica said that Gerry had been the one that had gone deeply into understanding the Swooshian diet and asked him to describe it.

Gerry said that the Swooshian diet was remarkably similar to that of whales or other creatures in the top of the food chain on Earth. They ate a variety of sea creatures similar to krill, shrimp, and sea bass.

He said that the majority of their food was grown and managed in areas of the ocean where food for them was plentiful. The growing areas were strategically located so the Swooshian members could swim into the thick soup of krill or shrimp and get their fill and then go on. He compared it to a gas station where one could drive through, and the gas would be sucked in by the grill of a car.

The Swooshians ate about once a day, and a meal consisted of about six thousand pounds of the krill or shrimp-like creatures. The shrimp like creatures were similar in size to the very large Vietnamese shrimp. When they were consumed the tonnage eaten was the same, but it could be consumed more quickly and would be considered "fast food" and was often consumed when a Swooshian was in a hurry to do something else.

He said he had learned that there were Swooshians that had stopped eating the krill, shrimp and the sea bass like fish and now exclusively survived on plankton. He said that they consumed around twelve tons of plankton a day.

He commented that he was impressed with the way the Swooshians attended to growing their food and arranging eating areas so that their population could be distributed throughout their water world. He made the point that food was basically a part of the way the society was managed and there was no "payment" for eating.

He commented that Earth could learn a lot about how to manage the growing of food, so the world population had easy and equal access to the food they needed.

Bram suggested the Mallica set the visit up but that she include Daryl Narda and Harold Redat who had actually searched many solar systems and found the water world. He then rattled off a set of names that he felt had also contributed.

He then asked Linda to arrange a celebratory meal that could be put in the two transport bubbles. He wanted Chef D'Carluca to be one of the guests on the visit.

That day at lunch, Chef D'Carluca came to his table and asked if they could meet some time after lunch.

Bram suggested that they meet after lunch whenever the Chef was ready. He said that he usually had Linda give him a ten-minute warning to let him closed down any other work he was doing.

In actuality he had set that process up when Einstein was with him so that he had time to put him away. That thought made him think that it was time for him to go back to his boulder in the desert to see if Einstein was still kicking.

Amy asked him if she, Pat, and Remi could meet with him sometime in the afternoon.

Bram suggested they contact Linda and get her to set up the meeting time and the amount of time they wanted.

Linda stopped him as he returned to his office. She said that she had booked time with the Chef and the meeting would start in fifteen minutes. She let him know that she had scheduled time with Amy and her group for about two hours later in the afternoon.

Bram thanked her and let her know that she should include herself on the Swooshian trip.

A few moments later Chef D'Carluca entered and looked around Bram's office and gave a whistle. He commented that it was his first time to see the office and he was impressed. He pointed to Zoe and Eric and smiled and said that he had not realized that they sat in the office all the time. He commented that there was also a small army outside the door.

He went on and said that he was surprised that Bram did not have a food taster to make sure his food was not poisoned.

Bram smiled and said that he had instead chosen to have the best Chef in the world to ensure his food was the best and poison free.

Chef D'Carluca bent his head and thanked him for the compliment. He then asked if it was true that it was appropriate for him to make a variety of sea food dishes for the feast to be consumed during the Fold to a Water world where the Aliens were Whalelike creatures.

Bram said that it was indeed appropriate because the primary food of these Aliens were krill, shrimp, fish, and seaweed.

Bram let Chef D'Carluca know that he was going to be the narrator of a brief presentation of each dish that would to be presented to the Swooshians. He suggested that the Chef choose to make any dish he wished to but that he should have a picture of the dish and then a picture of each ingredient in that dish so he could present it to the Swooshians.

Chef D'Carluca shook his head and said that he was a little off balance. He commented that he had just learned about the Aliens, he was going to make his first Fold trip, was being asked to prepare a celebration dinner, and have pictures to present.

He said he needed guidance and help.

He said that he had planned a Fold trip to La Spezia, on the Ligurian Sea, for the coming weekend. He wanted to understand how a Fold worked so that he would feel comfortable with the Fold to another world.

Bram said that he should enjoy his weekend in La Spezia. He was sure that Melisa had him staying in a great place. Bram said that he wanted to hear all about it on his return because he and Pat had talked about going there.

Fold Wormhole

He suggested that he give his request for help to Linda.

Linda called in her ten-minute warning.

The Chef got up and nodded and commented that Linda was indeed in charge of the work that went on in his office. He gave a salute to Linda as he went by her desk.

Remi led the way in and went to the fridge and took out a bottle of water and handed one to Pat and Amy.

Bram looked at the three and commented that they seemed to look serious.

Remi led the discussion. He commented that the three of them had been discussing how they might get Mataia ready to support the population at Einstein City and had decided that they needed guidance on how to approach terra forming their new world.

Amy added that they needed guidance on where to start and how to manage the timing and how to start with the most basic elements.

Pat then commented that she had contacted a group of scientists that were studying how to terra form Mars, and she had raised some basic questions about the process. She had been surprised by the knowledge of that group and was wondering if there might be great benefit for the Fold effort to engage with that group and work with them in how to terra form a new earth.

Bram looked at them and asked why they were in his office.

Remi smiled and said that they only wanted his money.

Bram asked how much they were planning to spend.

Pat said that they would most likely spend about a hundred thousand with the group of experts and then they would begin to spend somewhere between five hundred thousand to a million on gathering the various transformation plants, animals, and other transformation elements.

Bram nodded and said that as always money was not his concern. He was sure they would manage it wisely. He suggested they add Erica to their team and have her be the manager of the money and the three of them manage the terraforming.

Amy nodded and commented that the discussion had been easier than she had been expecting. She wondered if he had any concern about them making mistakes.

Bram nodded and said he was sure they would make mistakes as they made their move to a new world. He figured that they would manage the mistakes they made. He wished them a smooth terraforming experience.

He reminded them that they had talked about farming on Mataia and wondered how that fit in the terraforming plan they had in mind.

Pat said that they would keep that in mind when they got the guidance from the team they were engaging with.

He then asked Amy and Pat if they were interested in visiting a boulder in the desert.

Amy smiled and said that she had been curious about Einstein and what his family might look like.

Fold Wormhole

Bram said that he planned to Fold there and watch the Saturday morning sunrise from the boulder.

Pat and Amy both said they were in. Remi asked if he might go as well. He had not been to this boulder but had often heard about it.

Bram said they would meet at their six-person Fold craft at five in the morning. He would work with Marcus to make sure the coordinates would put them at the foot of the boulder.

At four in the morning Zoe was in the kitchen making coffee when Donna and Castor came in. She asked them how they had found out about the Saturday morning outing.

Castor said that a certain partner of hers had let them know. He said that he and Donna had worked on a ditty for them to chant on the jog in.

He then shared the ditty.

> *Going to the desert*
> *Going for the sunrise*
> *But not alone.*
> *Going back with a few*
> *Going to the desert*
> *We'll watch the sunrise.*
> *But not alone.*
> *Not alone*
> *Have hope to bring a certain someone home.*

Bram was surprised when he came down to the kitchen, but he had learned to accept the protective cover that was with him at all times.

He took Pat's hand and said it was time to go.

Linda and Castor led the way. Bob and Thomas followed them. Zoe and Eric brought up the rear.

Bram enjoyed the ditty and smiled as it was echoed across the grounds by the Marine guards.

Remi was standing at the six-person Fold vehicle when they arrived.

The Fold put them at the base of the boulder.

The black of the desert seemed formidable but the few steps from the Fold vehicle to the boulder was a way that Bram could do with his eyes closed. He led the group to the boulder and then climbed up and helped each of them up. He sat down in his usual spot. Pat was to his left and Amy and Remi were to his right.

They all sat in the dark that seemed to be a black comforter with millions of twinkling stars overhead providing the only light that allowed them to faintly see the rustling sage and tall grasses that surrounded them. A slight cool breeze put an edge to the morning, and they were all relieved to see the thin white line of the morning sun break along the horizon to the east.

Its slow steady approach was that of a black leopard moving stealthily in to capture its prey.

Bram watched as the sunlight slowly traveled toward them and then up the side of the boulder. It passed the opening from which Einstein had in the past always emerged. He wondered if Einstein was still around. He was just about to give up when Einstein appeared out of the hole on the side of the boulder.

Fold Wormhole

Bram opened the small container that held an oatmeal raison cookie.

Einstein came up to Bram and stood on his hind legs.

Bram put his open hand down and Einstein climbed in and then circled once and then curled up as he lay down.

After a moment Einstein climbed down and scurried down the boulder. Moments later he reappeared and was followed by four other mice.

Bram put his hand down and one at a time each mouse climbed into his hand and curled up and then climbed out.

Bram put down some cookie crumbs and they all ate some.

Then Einstein guided two of the mice up into Bram's palm.

Bram held his hand still and the two curled up and lay quietly.

Einstein turned and he and the other mouse climbed down to the hole in the side of the boulder and disappeared.

Bram carefully put the two mice into his jacket pocket. He understood that Einstein had given two of his own because he did not want one to be lonely as he had been.

It brought tears to his eyes. A simple mouse had shown more compassion than he had shown in the past.

Remi finally broke the silence by saying that if he had not just witnessed what he had with his own eyes he would never have believed it. Now he really believed that Einstein had been the one that had guided and Ok'd Bram's ideas.

Bram had his hand in his jacket pocket and could feel the two mice. He nodded and said he hoped that his two new helpers were as smart as their father had been. He was sure he needed the continuing coaching, and he now needed twice the help.

On his return he excused himself. He and Pat went to his office and took the two mice out of his pocket. He noted that one mouse had a black mark above its left eye. He asked Pat to help him name the two mice.

She lifted the tail of each mouse. She smiled and said that the one with the black spot should be named Isaac and the other should be named Ada after two famous scientists. They could both help him with the mathematical problems he would face dealing with both the negative and the positive universe.

He and Pat walked out to where everyone was waiting. Bram said he planned to jog back to the house, and he had a ditty for them to chant.

> *Went to the desert.*
> *Got Isaac and Ada*
> *Help in dealing with the law.*
> *Went to the desert.*
> *Learned compassion.*
> *Returned with a life's lesson.*
> *Went to the desert.*
> *Learned that life is more.*
> *More Than work*
> *More Than Play*
> *More to life in everyway*
> *Went to the desert.*
> *Got a reward.*

Bram knew that he was set for the next phase of his work.

The End

Chapter 1: Growing Old, Growing Bold

ℬram was going through his morning wake up preparation. He was standing in front of the mirror shaving and thinking about the "Negative Fold Universe." This was an accidental discovery made while he worked on what he now thought of as "The Positive Fold Universe" equation. He had been working on a way to move a Fold transport bubble in both the forward and reverse direction.

To go forward he had incremented time in each part of his Fold equation. He had done this by incrementing all the time components of the Fold equation in unison.

He discovered and had come to the realization that to go in reverse, he had to decrement time. This required one forward control program and a separate reverse control program.

Just as in an automobile both forward and reverse have different gearing. That was also true for the Fold equation. It took two separate programs that could not both be operating at the same time.

The oddity of the reverse equation was that once the Fold was back to its original start coordinate or zero start point, the equation kept going and operated on negative time. This is why he called it the Negative Fold Universe. He, however, had no understanding what the negative Fold equation represented.

The Earth that he had grown up on experienced time flowing from the point of the big bang that had created the universe out to infinity. He thought of it as flowing linearly from left to right.

He had not been able to determine how time was measured in the "Negative Fold Universe." He had now lost three bubble scouts and had no idea on how to retrieve them.

He was lost at how to maintain control of the bubbles entering the negative Fold zone.

He had come to the conclusion that he would need to personally go into the negative Fold realm to learn what was going on. He knew it was a risky thing to do but he felt that he would be able to figure out what was going on and make the adjustments that were needed to the negative Fold equation.

He had to try, and he had to do it alone.

This morning, he was carefully shaving and thinking about how he would handle the negative Fold universe and how to keep it invisible to the general population for the foreseeable future.

He suddenly stopped and stroked his hair back and realized that he had a streak of grey hair along the right side. He muttered a silent curse. Growing old was one of the few things that had not crossed his mind. He wondered how, when he was doing multiple Folds, he could possible develop grey hair. The Fold process had been proven to transform a person from a most deformed state to a perfect body and it had let him get grey hair!

Fold Wormhole

Pat entered and approached the second sink and saw Bram looking at his hair. She had meant to mention the grey to him but had been distracted by recent events and had forgotten. She reached up and let her fingers slide along the grey. She commented that it gave him the distinguished look of a wise man.

Bram smiled and thanked her and said that age unfortunately did not equate with wisdom.

He quietly finished shaving and let her know that he would be down getting a cup of coffee and then he was eager to get to work so he could tackle the conundrum of both wanting access to but wanting to keep everyone away from the negative Fold universe.

Pat spent a moment thinking up a ditty that the team could chant on the way into the work area compound. She smiled as she thought about the praise she had received about her ability to come up with good ditties, from Orlando, who was the master of coming up with ditties. He was the root of her current talent.

She thought for a few moments and thought she had a good one for this morning,

> *He's got a Silver streak, no he's not a freak*
> *He's growing old but growing bold*
> *I'm not too sure, It's what I am told*
> *Silver streak, no he's not a freak*
> *Growing old but growing bold*
> *Knows his way, through more than Fold*
> *Silver streak, no he's not a freak*
> *Growing old but growing bold*
> *Hi, Ho. Hi, Ho.*
> *No not growing old, just growing bold.*
> *Not too sure, it's what I'm told.*

She went to the kitchen for her coffee and enjoyed a slice of buttered toast with strawberry jam. She took a moment, jotted down the ditty, and handed it to Zoe letting her know that she should give it to Castor and Donna.

Zoe read the ditty and said she would be right back. She hustled down the stairs to the basement exit door and stepped out and handed Donna the ditty and said that they should use it this morning. She then returned to the kitchen just as Bram was rinsing out his cup.

Bram announced that it was time to go and led the way down the stairs to the basement exit.

When Castor and Donna said that they had a fresh ditty and took everyone through the first round, Bram smiled, he knew immediately who had written it. He looked at Pat and commented that she was getting as good as Orlando at writing ditties.

Zoe commented that Pat was better because she was closer and was able to ditty the most intimate occasions.

Pat laughed and said that she would limit her ditties to visually obvious things. The intimate parts were for her alone.

When Bram got to his office, Linda commented that for some reason he looked much more distinguished than she had previously noticed.

Bram smiled and shook his head and said she was looking much better than normal as well and wondered what make up she was wearing.

Fold Wormhole

Linda smiled and said she declared a truce and asked if they should start with setting up his two-week work schedule.

Bram replied that he wanted fifteen minutes and then they could set up the next two weeks.

He went in and started the pot for hot water.

He was followed in by his two FBI bodyguards, Zoe, and Eric.

Zoe asked if he was going to have tea or coffee. She would get the coffee ready if that was his choice.

Bram thanked her and chose coffee.

He then went to the bookshelf and opened the little door leading to the two mice he had returned with from the desert where they had visited the rock where he had sat for more than a year during the development of his Fold equation.

He had gone there to visit Einstein his pet mouse who had been his advisor during the development of the Fold equation and whom he had returned to the boulder a few months before.

On this visit Einstein had given him two of his offspring that he had brought back the day before.

Pat had helped him name the two. One was Isaac, named after a famous scientist and the other, Ada, was named after another famous scientist. They both came out and got into his hand. Bram carried them to his desk and put them down at the center of the picture of the milky way. This picture was the size of his desk and was under the class covering.

It was the picture that had captured his imagination when he was a young boy, and it had drawn him into the field that he was now pursuing.

He quietly told the two mice that he was going to ask for their help to set up the way to handle the negative universe the way that their father had helped him set up the Fold equation.

He smiled and pointed to them and said that they had both agreed by shaking their heads in the affirmative.

Zoe brought over his coffee and petted each of the mice with her finger and then put down some cookie crumbs.

Bram smiled and asked if she were trying to take his job or replace his relationship with his new advisors.

Zoe shook her head and said that she did not want a silver streak in her hair and that she would stick with dodging bullets and taking on the bad guys and he could go grey thinking about the Fold world.

Bram responded that he thought maybe the grey streak was a result of worrying about her tweaking his nose while he was deep in thought.

He then looked down to Isaac and Ada and told them that they now saw the stress he was constantly in because of this one bodyguard.

Eric brought over two more small cookie crumbs. He asked if the cookie was all that they got to eat.

Fold Wormhole

Bram took Isaac and Ada back to the little door and they scurried in. He then opened the two doors below the main bookshelf and showed Eric the automated food and water set up that supplied the two mice with what they needed.

Isaac and Ada could be seen on the open side of the feeder taking a few nibbles.

He commented that the two had a fairly extensive tube system that also went outside where they could catch the morning sun.

He commented that there was even a transport tube that went to the Viewing Room and that it had been installed when the room was Zuri's office back when she needed the room for her wheelchair.

Eric said that he was impressed. He had wondered about Einstein and how he had lived while he was still with Bram.

Bram commented that he felt a little remorseful about having kept Einstein alone for so long. He said that Einstein had sent him a clear message by having him take two of his kids back with him.

He then smiled and said he hoped that the two were as smart as their father.

Zoe shook her head and said it was a little disconcerting to think that he was getting affirmation for his ideas from mice.

Bram smiled and said that he found the little creatures very critical to his thinking.

Linda knocked, entered, and said that his fifteen-minute reprieve was up, and it was time to work on his two-week work calendar.

Bram nodded and said that there was no escaping his responsibilities while she was around.

After spending almost an hour getting the next two weeks organized, Bram asked Linda to arrange for Marcus and Remi to meet with him. He suggested the ten o'clock open period on his calendar. He also asked her to see if Pat and Amy would be available for an afternoon trip to Mataia.

He asked Zoe and Eric if they needed to be with him on the Fold to Mataia.

Zoe commented that now that he had proven that he could get to the future it meant they could reach back into the past. This meant he needed more protection, not less.

Bram asked what she meant.

Zoe commented that unknown to any of them, he might have some enemy in the future that might take some sort of action against him. They should be ready for such an eventuality.

Bram nodded and then he smiled and said he agreed but he really felt that those in the future should love him and regard him as a scientific hero.

Zoe nodded and said that was exactly how everyone in their current time period should feel but it seemed that some of those that did not love him were willing to try to kill him.

Fold Wormhole

Bram commented that they would need to rethink their current protection procedure and make sure they thought about an attack from some group from the future. He commented that they should put this discussion on the calendar and get General Tilson and Lacy in on the conversation.

Zoe suggested they do it sooner and not later because she had a bad feeling about the future.

Linda announce the arrival of Marcus and Remi, who walked in and welcomed him back from his trip to Gabon. Remi asked if they had ended up with a friendly new member on the Oversight Committee.

Bram commented that he felt great about the trip and about having an Oversight Committee that would be supportive overall of the Fold effort.

He then let them know that what he wanted to do now was to make the negative Fold capability invisible to the world for the foreseeable future. He wanted them to visit Mataia and determine what they needed to do to establish a center where everything about negative Fold would be located. He wanted to set up a work center that was harder to get in or out of than Fort Knox. He made the point that the negative Fold capability was worth more than all the wealth of their world and when that became known they would all be in danger.

He pointed out that it also was the ying and yang of the world of the good and the bad. He shared what Zoe had said about not everyone loving him. He did not understand why that was the case but as she had pointed out he was not allowed to go anywhere without someone attacking him. She had challenged him and asked him if he thought everyone in the future would love him.

Remi looked at Zoe and commented that he had seen her in action and that Bram should listen to her carefully.

Bram said that he had listened and was going to review all the protection systems and protocols that they had set up and add the threat from the future as a new complication.

He said that he would have Linda set up a session with General Tilson and Lacy for the following day. He said that they should all plan to attend and bring their attack from the future scenarios to share.

Marcus commented that he was going to ask his kids about an attack from the future and how it would be carried out. He said that he would make it a game and see what they would come up with.

Bram said that sounded like a great idea. He then added, "from the mouths of babes."

He then took the two into the objective of the meeting and that focused on setting up the negative Fold work area on Mataia.

Marcus and Remi both agreed and threw in their ideas about the design of the work center.

Fold Wormhole

When it came time for lunch, he called it quits, and they went to the cafeteria.

Amy and Pat were sitting together when they spotted Bram coming in for lunch. Pat commented that his protectors were all acting as if danger were close at hand. Amy looked around the sparsely populated cafeteria and said that she did not see any threats.

Pat knew that Zoe had commented that the threat level had risen, but she had not volunteered any information but had commented that she would soon have Bram working on better protection.

Bram walked over to Pat and said that he was looking forward to going to Mataia after lunch and was that something that could possibly be made to happen. He was about to go and get his lunch when Chef D'Carluca brought out a dish that he said he was perfecting that he called Swooshian Spaghetti di Mare and that he wanted to have Bram be the first to try it and give him feedback.

He looked around the table and asked if anyone else wanted to be a judge of his latest creation.

Everyone raised a hand.

He smiled. He commented that he had been counting on Bram making everyone hungry. He said that he would have the plates sent out.

Zoe commented that she was glad that she was on duty and that she would have hated to have missed out on one of the Chef's latest creations.

She commented that one of the benefits of guarding Bram was that he had exciting fishing trips that always seemed to feature fireworks, exciting vacations that had missiles and semi's trying to blow them up and a Chef that loved to try new dishes out on him.

Castor said that he had to fight off other Marines in order to keep his current assignment when they had found out he got to feast on Chef D'Carluca's special dishes.

Bram laughed and said that other than dealing with explosions and dodging lead, their work was a piece of cake.

Chef D'Carluca's Swooshian Spaghetti di Mare was a truly delicious spaghetti made with baby clams, mussels, squid, and shrimp in a thick dark blue sauce. He explained that the blue color came diluted from squid ink.

Everyone complimented him and said that once again he was pushing the limits of extremely great flavor.

After lunch Castor and Linda led the way to the hanger where the six-person Fold vehicle was waiting.

The Fold into the Mataia Arrival Terminal was uneventful.

Fold Wormhole

Bram described that he was looking to house the negative Fold effort as well as to house the vehicle or vehicles that would be limited to use in the negative Fold realm. He shared that he was planning on having a special vehicle that would hold ten with ten beds and a supply of food that would hold them for a month. He made the point that he was not planning any long forays into the negative Fold realm, but he was going to be prepared for any unplanned problem.

Pat looked at Amy and said that the empty hangar capable of holding Wheel One had plenty of space. She pointed out that a multilevel work center could be added. She said that the first level would be the Launch-Return site. They could equip that level with Sterile holding areas that would be isolated. The floor above it could hold a large lab. The third floor could be a large work center.

Amy commented that if the structure was located at the far end and the top two levels had windows to the external three sides they could make it feel very much like the work floor in the main Mataia Fold work building.

Bram asked Amy to walk off the area she was thinking about. After she had done this Bram asked to walk around the exterior of the hangar. He wanted to get a feel for the view, but he was also interested on how protection could be integrated into the building.

Once he had made the walk he asked Pat and Amy to join in on the meeting of Zoe, the General and Lacy to discuss how to make what they built as secure as his current office.

Amy thanked him and commented that she would take what she learned into consideration and have his office in the main Mataian building modified to have the same level of protection. She commented that protection had been overlooked when they built Einstein City and that she and Pat would take a cut at making sure they reviewed all the structures that Bram would frequent.

Bram thanked her and commented that every home and building should have a saferoom and they would need to experiment to see if they could set up a system that would prevent anyone from Folding into the safe rooms. He commented that making a Fold proof save room was going to be a challenge.

The next day during the meeting that focused on reviewing the safety protocol, Marcus said that his kids had come up with a variety of ideas that he would never have thought about.

One of their suggestions was to set up a laser screen around the perimeter of the room and test to see if Folding in was possible. They suggested that the laser screen should be similar to the screen on the porch screen door.

The second suggestion was to have a laser weapon that would sweep the room on a multilevel that was strong enough to cut someone into pieces.

He said another suggestion was to have a system that shot spikes up from the floor that were only inches apart.

The General laughed and asked what Marcus was feeding his kids.

Marcus said that he was always surprised by what his kids could come up with and that they were eating healthy meals.

Bram said that he would investigate each of their suggestions but the laser to cut people into pieces and shooting up spikes from the floor seemed to be out on the edge of what he had in mind.

He asked he General if he had any other better suggestions.

The General said, "touche" and then went on and suggested that they set up an armed bubble protection system on Mataia. He said he had two Marine's that needed to be promoted and who he did not want to lose. He could promote them and assign them to operate the protection bubble system on Mataia. They would still be housed on Earth, but they would always activate the bubble system on Mataia ahead of Bram and make sure the area was clear before his arrival.

Bram complemented the General and said that he thought that his suggestion should be implemented as soon as possible. He said that he would immediately begin to work on the laser screen suggestion that Marcus's children had made. He was thinking the screen should be a laser screen that as it sliced an object up would send each piece to separate random distances in negative space.

The General looked at Pat and asked what she was feeding Bram.

She smiled and said that Bram had the talent to take a simple idea and make it into a horror movie scene.

She then added that it was not what she was feeding him, but he was just seeing the side of Bram that she feared the most.

Amy joined in and commented that had she known about the Bram dark side she would have left him in the desert.

Bram stood up and bowed and said that he was ending the meeting on that note and planned to walk home slowly and absorb the painful feedback he had just received.

The General laughed and said he now knew how to quickly end meetings with him.

Chapter 2: Future Surprise

Bram began a head on attack to figure out how to gain control of the negative Fold universe. He knew that he needed to take an aggressive approach, and he needed to do it quickly before the Fold technology became known in his time. He read through several diverse fields dealing with the universe and reviewed competing theories. This led him to believe that the interaction of black matter, gravity, light, distance, and the expansion speed of the universe were all involved in creating the phenomena of a universe where time flowed both in a linear fashion from the big bang to infinity as well as the same universe where distance seemed to dictate the size of a rhombicosidodecahedron (RCID) where time was not measurable but inferred by the node sequence of the RCID. He was convinced that the greater the initial Fold distance the farther back in time the traveler would find themselves.

He personally had experienced that effect.

The way back from such a "time distance" was to jump from one RCID node to the next node in a given sequence for thousands, or perhaps millions of nodes. This in the linear universe he lived in would take an unmeasurable amount of time. He figured that most likely there was a way to choose what the next point on the RCID would be but currently he had no clue how to accomplish this.

As he reviewed the various papers that had been published on the measurement of distance across the universe and of the changing knowledge of how fast the universe was expanding the more convinced he was that the negative Fold environment was the result of the interactions happening similar to the interaction in his current time on the subatomic particle level. At that level, in the positive Fold world, it appeared that time did not exist. The negative Fold universe was a macro example of the same phenomena. Time did not exist in the negative Fold realm.

This was a concept that Bram found perplexing, but he figured that he would slowly work his way through until he understood the negative Fold universe. He likened it to the slow pace at which he had learned the Swooshian language.

He was convinced that what he had experienced in his first venture into the negative Fold universe was that distance had a similar attribute to time in his universe and he wondered if the measure of distance was linear from the big bang and followed the expansion speed of the universe.

Fold Wormhole

The only thing that had saved him was the light that Pat had sent out with the old-fashioned Morse code that gave him a visual shortcut back to the time that he had entered the negative Fold realm. This meant that light was linear in the negative Fold realm and acted independently to both distance and time.

As he continued his studies it became apparent to him that the expansion of the Universe, the effects of gravity on light, the effects of gravity on matter and the fact that time did not exist, all interacted to produce a realm where reality was not the simple solid touch something and you knew it was real that was true in the positive Fold universe where time began with the big bang and existed as a constantly moving event.

He used the Bayesian inference statistical method and used all the elements he thought were pertinent to create a model of how nonexistent time affected where a negative Fold vehicle would end up. Once he had the model, he created a computer control program for one of the negative Fold bubbles.

He then needed to test how his Fold bubble moved in the negative Fold universe.

He engaged Marcus and together they began a series of trials and after several Fold trips they were able to recognize that the resulting location was based on the initial time settings in the Fold vessels control computer.

The time in the control settings seemed to interact with gravity and the black matter through which the Fold vessel traveled. Using his model, he reconstructed the gravity of the

Universe throughout cosmic history in a computer model based on all the parameters including the positive Fold sections.

Bram realized that they were developing an equation that they could learn to manipulate not by brilliantly thinking through the model but by using plain old-fashioned trial and error experimentation. Each trial resulted in another increment of learning that allowed him to try yet another tweak of the model. This meant that he would be able to use his statistical model to continue tweaking the Fold equation and exploring the limits of traveling in the negative Fold realm.

Marcus commented that they were slow learners on how to handle how far the send journey would be and it was the light beacon that Pat had set up that allowed them to always retrieve the negative Fold vessel successfully.

Bram agreed and said that Pat had provided the practical tool that was going to allow them to slowly map the Negative Fold realm.

Both of them had been doing their work from their workspace in the new lab on Mataia as they waited for their new work area in the Mataia hangar to be built. Bram's bodyguards were with them at all times. Bram had made it a point that each day they Fold back to Earth for lunch.

It was Zoe that noticed that Bram's grey streak had disappeared, and she commented that she had figured out why Bram had suggested Folding back for lunch.

Fold Wormhole

Bram chuckled because he had not noticed the change until Zoe joked about it. He put it down to the positive side effect of Folding. His team all had a list of ailments that they no longer suffered. He knew that his first mouse Einstein was living much longer than any mouse he knew about.

He speculated that somewhere in the future a huckster would be selling Fold trips with the claim that it would heal any ailment. As he thought about it he knew that more experimentation on that side effects of Folding was needed.

Pat had taken the lead in the ultimate transformation that took Zuri from her wheelchair through a phenomenal body transformation. Zuri was currently nearing the end of her time attending Oxford. She had moved universities from the one that accepted her in her wheelchair and had gone to Oxford where no one knew she had been wheelchair bound for all her life. She was a Fold miracle.

Zoe observed Bram thinking and figured he had come up with yet another project. She had learned to read the moments when Bram hit on a new thought. She had never told him that he would close his eyes and when he opened them, smile, and nod to himself.

Bram realized that his protection team was waiting for him to disembark the Fold vehicle. He had been lost in envisioning how therapeutic Folds should be managed. He would ask Pat to take the lead and organize that area.

Pat sat at the table with Amy. They were both looking forward to the usual team lunch. They had just completed the entire structure that would be the Negative Fold work building on Mataia. The entire structure had been built on a slab next to the Fruit Barn Production area on Earth. It would be Folded into location by the end of the week. They needed to work with Marcus so they could Fold it into the precise location at the end of the hangar.

She and Amy had already removed the section of the hanger on Mataia that would be filled by the new section they had just finished. The final finishing touches would be done by the workers that were currently finishing the interior of the building. She was pleased with the openness of the building's negative Fold work area. She knew that Bram would spend a great deal of time there and she wanted it to be a comfortable place with an outstanding view.

She was aware that Bram had developed a very sophisticated laser barrier system based on the suggestion of Mylan and Marcus Jr.

The grid to prevent any unsolicited Folds into the building would be implemented immediately after the building was moved into place. The shield was an amazing laser grid that would wrap around the entire building. Anything passing through it would be sliced into tiny pieces that were then randomly Folded into negative space.

Fold Wormhole

She knew that Bram had worked independently on the program and planned to locate the transmitter in a location only he knew about. It was his way of making it almost impossible for the future to interfere with the past.

She had the feeling that the transmitter would not be on Mataia but some undisclosed location and would have its own power system and would not need any attention.

She was aware that Bram had a Fold vehicle built that he was outfitting on his own. He let her know that no one would be allowed to see what was in it or to know where it was located. He said that it would also hold all the current knowledge of the Negative and the Positive Fold realms. He said that should he die, the information would be released a few centuries later.

She knew that he was trying to protect the entire human species as well as their Water World intelligent beings.

As Bram walked into the cafeteria, he looked over at where Pat and Amy were sitting and knew by their smiles that they had good news. He had been following the work they had been doing to get the Fold work center on Mataia built and knew they were close to completion. He had purposely stayed away from the area where they were having it built. Instead, he had focused his efforts on setting up the anti-intruder laser grid.

He had recruited Erica to obtain a series of laser transmitters that could be set up to create a fly screen pattern around the entire work center. The power required to operated it was substantial and he worked with Remi to build a Fold vessel that would be able to generate the power needed and be able to keep the shield activated from a remote location.

He sat down and took a few bites of the slice of rare top loin roast that he was dipping in a sauce that Chef D'Carluca had insisted he try. The sliced fried green tomatoes were his effort at making sure he had a vegetable on his plate.

He looked at Amy and asked if she had crashed one of the Hilos.

She shook her head and asked why he would ask such a question.

He smiled and said that he observed that she was fidgeting and closely watching him eat.

Pat said that the two of them were excited to be able to announce that the negative Fold structure would be Folded into place on the following day and then they would have the structure activated three days later. He would then be able to activate his anti-intruder laser grid.

Bram complimented them at the speed at which they were setting up the structure and getting it into place. He said that he had focused on a much simpler effort and was lagging behind the timing they were achieving. He said that he would have to put the shield grid back on the front burner so that he could immediately activate it when they had the building in place

He added that he wanted to prevent the future from putting in any monitoring or spying devices. He wanted a clean work area.

Pat commented that she figured that he would be far ahead of any action the future might take.

Bram shook his head and replied that he was hoping that speed would at least keep him in the lead.

Zoe felt a shiver run down her back. She spoke softly to Eric and said that they should be prepared. Eric knew immediately that Zoe had experienced one of her intuitive moments and was now in an activated high adrenaline state. It was the same when they were getting on the car ferry on the trip through Norway.

She had the premonition then and her swift actions had saved them. The two of them had discussed these feelings she got and how they had always been accurate.

He had no idea what had caused her to feel that way, but he had come to know that she was correct one hundred percent of the time.

Eric excused himself and said he would return shortly. He left and went to a locker outside of Bram's office where they kept their Kevlar jackets and high-power weapons. He took all the weapons and protective equipment for all four of them out to the Fold craft. He laid the gear out for each of them and then returned to the cafeteria. He got there as Bram was getting ready to return to Mataia.

As he and Zoe got ready to take the lead back to the Fold vehicle, he let Thomas and Bob know that he had moved all their gear to the Fold craft, and they needed to be ready for action.

He then let Castor and Donna know they should be ready for action and did they need to stop anywhere to get their gear.

Castor shook his head, patted his backpack, and said they never went anywhere without their tools. He said that they were at full readiness.

Bram sensed that the atmosphere had changed. He likened it to the dip in atmospheric pressure just before a storm. He observed that his bodyguards were silent. When they got to the craft to get in each of his FBI bodyguards put on their Kevlar jackets and positioned their weapons at their seats.

Zoe handed him his vest and asked him to put it on. He did as she asked. He had his own weapon under his seat. He took it out, placed it and the extra ammo clip within reach as he sat down in the Fold vessel. He asked Zoe what was up.

Fold Wormhole

He was not surprised that she simply replied, "premonition." This was the same as her reply to Matt when he had asked how she knew the truck in the tunnel was a trap and a bomb.

Remi and Marcus were both with him and it was clear to him that they had not picked up on the change in atmosphere. They were talking about the huge difficulty of figuring out the coordinates to place a building on a planet going through space and how Marcus had worked with Pat and Amy to place it exactly plus or minus one half inch within the rectangle represented by those coordinates.

Bram asked them to remain to the back of the team when they got to Mataia.

Their arrival to the Mataian Arrival-Departure Terminal was normal. Amy insisted on checking the terminal before allowing the rest of the team to disembark.

Their walk from the terminal up to Remi's lab was a little slower and Bram was surrounded by his bodyguards but otherwise it was uneventful.

Bram wondered if Zoe's intuition was off.

When they got to the lab door, Zoe put her open hand up and her finger of her other hand to her pursed lips. She then started a loud conversation with herself as she approached the door. She opened it fast and dove in toward the left and Eric followed and dove to the right. Castor and Linda dove straight in and slid on their stomachs with their back packs in front of them.

At first the silence made Bram think that Zoe had overreacted but then the continuous roar coming through the door seemed to be that of several large gatling guns firing simultaneously, and the area sounded like a full war zone. Thomas and Bob had pushed him to the wall and were trying to shielding him.

He pushed past them with his gun drawn and entered, turned to the right, and immediately shot two armed persons who were attacking his bodyguards from the side. The bodyguards had their attention toward their front and had not seen the attackers.

Bram continued along the wall firing at the attacking fighters. Then he took down two more when he was able to shoot behind the shields they were holding. He ran toward the other side of the room as he changed to a new bullet clip. He then fired from the side and shot the remaining fighters.

Once the shields fell, the barrage from Zoe, Eric, Castor, and Donna took down the wounded fighters.

He was glad that he had supported Zoe's anticipation of trouble and had put on his Kevlar vest because he had felt the hits as he crossed the room during the fight. He had been hit several times and was sure he would later feel the pain but at the moment his adrenaline was serving its purpose.

He watched as Zoe walked up to two wounded attackers and shot them. The grim look on her face warned him not to say a word. She checked to make sure the other attackers were dead. She commented that only dead assassins would be sent back to the future.

Fold Wormhole

He noted that Eric had gathered the attackers' weapons and was putting then into one of the steel chests. He wondered why and was about to ask when a loud explosion caused the chest to lose its shape and look more like a stainless-steel sausage.

He asked Eric how he had known that the weapons would blow up.

Eric replied that he hadn't known but that he and Zoe had discussed what to expect if the future came back to attack them. They had agreed that the weapons would most likely self-destruct, so that the past could not gain knowledge about the future weapons technology.

They had also discussed the fact that in a conflict the future would expect to win and would come in a group they felt would be sufficient to quickly overcome their adversaries.

Bram suggested they search for a Fold vessel.

Zoe commented that it was not in their time but would potentially Fold in to pick up the attackers. She asked that they all stay close to the wall while she walked around and checked out the lab. She got down and glanced along the floor and on top of the larger worktables.

She pointed to the four chairs at each of the four tables and said that the attackers had sat on the stools with their weapons at the ready and shields besides them. She went to the largest open lab area and said that the Fold craft from the future had sat down, and the attackers had all gotten out, then the craft had Folded away.

She squatted down and pointed to one of the tiles that had some scuff marks on it and commented when they had the time, they would be able to match the scuff mark material to some of the boots on the attackers.

Bram asked Castor if he had any grenades with him. The lab was silent for a moment.

Then both Linda and Castor commented that they always carried several grenades with them.

Bram asked if they knew how to booby trap the bodies so that the future would receive a reply to their attack that they were probably not expecting.

He said that they as a team should not say another word about the attack so that the future would not know about the surprise they were about to get.

Zoe smiled and commented that how to behave was getting more complicated by the moment. She asked for everyone to help her get the bodies ready to take a trip to the future.

Bram watched as Castor placed his four grenades on four bodies and Donna did the same. It was clear to him that Castor had done it before in actual battle conditions and that Donna was watching Castor, so she placed and handled her grenades that same way.

Fold Wormhole

Castor said that he would wire all of them together once they got them into their Fold vehicle. He would then attach the wire to the door. He explained the grenades would explode the moment the door was opened. He was not sure about the strength of the Fold vessel, but the open doorway would provide a way that he could launch a cloud of shrapnel. He looked around and asked if they had shrapnel that they could use.

Bram asked Remi what he had in the lab that they could gather to fill a container with, to put in the doorway.

Remi and Marcus went around opening drawers and cabinets and filling a trash can with a variety of metal lab tools and threw in glassware that broke. They carried back a large plastic trashcan full of the mix of glass and a variety of lab tools that included a set of knives and some tools that looked as if they belonged in a horror movie.

Zoe got everyone to stand against the wall while they waited for the Fold vessel from the future to appear.

Bram smiled when it Folded in. The vessel was still the same basic u-tube design that they were currently using. It made him wonder how close in the future his attackers were. He figured it might be close to his hundred-year Fold time capsule.

He watched as the team loaded the bodies and Castor and Linda worked together to wire all the grenades together.

He took a quick walk through the craft. He looked into the various packs and found several computer-looking devices. He did not recognize the brands but knew that the future was close enough that the technology was still recognizable. He handed the computers to Marcus and said they were souvenirs that he could study.

Marcus had been silent for the whole time, he said that he would love to fire them up and see what they would learn. He suggested that they should first figure out how to copy the memory. He said that they would most likely spend some time using the supercomputer to get past any passwords or whatever the lock to the computer would be.

Bram nodded and said they would all participate in breaking into the computers from the future.

Bram pointed to the forward single seat and said that it seemed to be the control or pilots seat. He noted what he took as the Fold button and suggested they put a weight over it that they could cause to fall and initiate the Fold back to the future.

Castor took a heavy piece of metal and put a set of folded paper matches to hold it up over the button. He said that they would have about thirty seconds after he lit the matches before the heavy piece of metal fell on the button.

Everyone got out and stood against the wall.

Castor lit the matches, closed the Fold craft's door got against the wall and when his count got to the word "thirty" the craft disappeared.

Fold Wormhole

He said he would love to be able to see if their return gift caused the damage, he was hoping it would.

Bram commented that it might just be possible, but he still had some complicated analysis and experimenting that he would need to do. He let the team know that if it ever became possible to travel to the future, he would see about arranging such a Fold for all of them. He commented that until he was able to block the future, they should all standby for the attacks from the future versus the attacks during fishing.

Bram had overlooked that the attacks on the lake could just as well come from the future as well as from the current time.

Continue the story in: ***The Negative Fold***

Ron Mueller

Fold Wormhole

<u>About the Author</u>

Ronald E. Mueller
remwriter95@gmail.com
    Ron grew up in what is now Flint River State Park in Southeast Iowa. The 170-year-old house Ron lived in is built into a hillside. It faces a 125-foot-high cliff towering over the little Flint River. The house and the land talked to him about; the passing of time, the struggle to conquer the land, the struggles people faced and the wonder of nature.

He climbed the cliffs, crawled into the caves, dove from the swimming rock, collected clams from the bottom of the pond, gigged and skinned frogs for their legs. He trapped muskrats for fur, hunted raccoon in the dead of night, and with only a stick hunted rabbits in the dead of winter.

His young life was outdoors, and nature tested him.

He walked to a one room stone schoolhouse uphill both ways. A stern but warm-hearted teacher, Mrs. Henry was instrumental in shaping his character as she shepherded him from the fourth to the eighth grade. A Montessori before its time. It was a great way to grow up.

His experiences inter-twined with snippets of fantasy lend themselves to the adventures he leads the reader through.

Fold Characters

Amy	Wellington	NASA astronaut
Aanon	Zann	Swoosh Leader of the Alien's
Ada	Mouse	Einstein's children mice
Angela	Newton	Olivia Newton's Daughter
Bob		FBI bodyguards
Bonank	Etaing	Senator Senate Oversight Committee
Bram	Nielson	Protagonist
Castor	Suarez	Marine guard
Cedric	Stetson	Fishing boat
Celilo	Park	Fishing launch area, along Columbia River.
Charles	Ford	Science Advisor Senate Oversight Committee
Dalles		site in Oregon along Columbia River.
Danial	Bascom	Senator W Virginia Senate Oversight Committee
Daryl	Nazda	Backup Pilot Bubble 1 Pat Pilot
David	Conden	Utah Senator's partner
Dennison	Newton	Olivia Newton's Son
Donna		New Marine guard
Edward	Sharp	Site Marine Commander
Einstein	Mouse	Bram's first mouse
Einstein City		City on the Mataia
Elizabeth	Miller	humanist philosopher, .
Eric		FBI bodyguards
Erica	Wilson	Initial archrival
Ester	Mannerly	Nasa quality inspector for the two wheels.
Gerald	Gerry	Sooner Captain Erica's husband
Harold	Redat	Backup Pilot Bubble 2 Amy Pilot
Isaac	Mouse	Einstein's children mice
Jeffrey	Mikelson	Boss that is patient,
Jina	Juma	Mom
John	Morgan	NASA director Jefferies Boss
John	Stately	Senator Utah Senate Oversight Committee
Jose	Estrada	project manager wheel one and two
Lacy	Stetson	first office support. Ted's daughter

Fold Wormhole

Lester	Tilson	Marine Major General in charge of Fold security
Linda	Stetson	Ted's oldest becomes Bram's support.
Lori	Middleton	Lab, workshop supervisor
Luke	Stetson	Fishing boat Ted's son
Mallica	Evenston	World class mathematician
Marcus	Smith	World class astrophysicist
Marial	Stetson	Brought Picnic lunch, Cedric's wife
Mary		Rushing River Inn Owner
Mataia	(Ma ta ee ah)	New world to which Bram moves
Melisa	Etrius	Organizer of the Fold neighborhood activities
Mike		Rushing River Inn Owner
Mt. Jefferson		hike & fishing, near to Rushing River
Myla	Smith	
Nuro	Juma	Dad
Ohaan	Toon	Bram's Alien equivalent
Olivia	Newton	Senator Maine Senate Oversight Committee
Orlando	Gutieres	Marine guard
Patricia	Fleming	NASA astronaut Bram's mate
Primeira	Planet	New Dry world to be used
Raymond		Daedlus Husband to be of Lacy
RCID		Rhombicosidodecahedron, Geometric shape
Remi	Hardwood	Direct bubble assembly Lab technical
rhombicosidodecahedron		RCID shape of time & distance in neg Fold
Rita	Stetson	Brought Picnic lunch - Ted's wife
Samuel	Natorly	US President
Serena	Windal	Fold phycologist -Marine Therapist
Swoosh	Water Planet	Name of Alien Water world
Ted	Stetson	Fishing boat
Thomas		FBI bodyguards
USS Hood Wheel One		First Fold vessels
USS Rainier Wheel Two		First Fold vessels
Woo-an	Ang	Ohaan's mate
Zoe		FBI bodyguards
Zuri	Juma	Wheelchair bound autistic mental giant

Ron Mueller

Published by: Around the World Publishing LLC.

QR Links to

ATWP.US web site

* 9 7 8 1 6 8 2 2 3 2 7 5 0 *